Don't Walk On My Dreams

A Novel

by

Annie Greene Nelson

THE REPRINT COMPANY, PUBLISHERS
SPARTANBURG, SOUTH CAROLINA
1976

This volume was reproduced from a 1961 edition.

Reprinted: 1976
The Reprint Company, Publishers
Spartanburg, South Carolina

ISBN 0-87152-245-4
Library of Congress Catalog Card Number: 76-18308
Manufactured in the United States of America on long-life paper.

Library of Congress Cataloging in Publication Data

Nelson, Annie Greene.
    Don't walk on my dreams.

    Reprint , with new introd., of the ed. published
by the author, Columbia, S. C.
    I. Title.
PZ3.N329Do5 [PS3527.E372] 813'.5'2 76-18308
ISBN 0-87152-245-4

INTRODUCTION

The publication of *After the Storm* in 1942 marked a first in South Carolina literary and publishing history: its author, Annie Greene Nelson, became the first black woman in the state to write and publish a novel. The limited edition was quickly sold out. The success of her first book encouraged Mrs. Nelson to publish a second, *The Dawn Appears,* in 1944, again with rapid success. A number of years elapsed before the publication, in 1961, of *Don't Walk on My Dreams.*

Despite the acclaim granted Mrs. Nelson in recent years, these books are rare on library shelves because of the limited numbers in which they were printed. *After the Storm* and *The Dawn Appears* were originally published in editions of 500 copies each by the Hampton Publishing Company, which also printed the early black newspaper in South Carolina, *The Palmetto Leader.* By the time *Don't Walk on My Dreams* was written, Hampton Publishing Company had been sold, and Mrs. Nelson undertook the publication of her third novel herself, again in a limited edition of 500 copies.

For the author, the publication of these books represented the culmination of an ambition which had begun to take shape for her many years earlier as a child in Darlington County, in the Pee Dee section of South Carolina. The oldest of thirteen children, Annie Greene was born into a life that contained its share of hardship. Her father was a farmer who worked on a number of plantations in the Darlington area and she grew up with what would have seemed to be little prospect of success. But her father was determined that his children would know how to read: he taught her, and she read everything she could get her hands on. Then, in early childhood, she had an experience that changed her life: "I was left one evening near a wood, in a cotton field," she recalls. "I looked around, and I saw little colored moons everywhere, moving all around me. I wasn't afraid: I just watched, and then they went off. It was like Joseph's dream about the sun and the moon and the eleven stars bowing down to him. I felt as if I had been picked out for something special, and I came out of that cotton field determined to make something of myself."

With her sights set on being a school teacher, Annie Greene graduated from the Darlington County schools, went to Benedict College for two years, and then attended and graduated from Voorhees College with a degree in education and nursing. She taught in the schools of Darlington, Lexington, and Richland counties. When she married, she settled in Columbia.

The desire to do something special persisted. "I always had a high ambition," she says. "I was determined not to suffer like so many I saw." But the suffering she had witnessed among her people led to a feeling that she had to put into words the deprivations, the fears, the joys, and the abiding courage of her race. In 1942, while keeping house and caring for her children, Mrs. Nelson sat down and wrote *After the Storm*. It was written in two nights and is the story of someone she knew very well. *The Dawn Appears* and *Don't Walk on My Dreams* reflect a number of incidents about several people. "Every one is a true story," she says, "just with different names." The three books are not in any way tied together, but all reflect the continuity of her own experience, observations, and beliefs.

Other works by Mrs. Nelson followed *After the Storm* and *The Dawn Appears*. *Shadows of the Southland* was serialized in *The Palmetto Leader* in 1952. A play by Mrs. Nelson, "Happenings on the Parrott's Plantation," is being performed in Darlington. She has just completed her autobiography, entitled *To Paw with Love,* a book in the form of letters written to her father at home in Darlington County.

Her books are "affectionately dedicated" to the Pee Dee section of South Carolina, and portray the lives of the black inhabitants of the region. She treats with insight and compassion the sufferings, courage, and eventual triumph of a young girl deceived by her fiance; the experience of Negro soldiers preparing to fight in defense of a country they believed in although it had not always treated them well; the understanding and cooperation between white landlords and black workers on the plantation; customs, celebrations, and beliefs among Southern black people at home; the importance of religion and revivals in black culture; birth, family life, and death in the midst of hardship; and the struggle for dignity and education in the midst of toil and subservience.

"All my life I have been a close observer of things," she says. Her writings are a mixture of general experience, of stories related to her, and the lives of those around her. She has heard many stories of sad and terrible events, and witnessed much suffering. She remembers her baby brother burning to death in front of her eyes when she was scarcely two years old. She heard half-whispered stories of lynching, murder, and cruelty. But she remembers good times as well—happy times on the Parrott's plantation among kind white people—and stories spiced with humor. The story of her great-grandmother, Mary Berry, who as a child was kidnapped from her native land and sold into slavery, was told to her by Mary Berry herself. And the memory of her father's love for her and ambition for his children is an important part of her life.

Annie Greene Nelson today is a pert, dapper woman with a youthful appearance and attitude. She lives in Columbia, South Carolina, with her husband Ed Nelson. She has six children, one of whom has an earned doctorate and teaches at LaValle University in Canada. Two daughters teach school, one in South Carolina, and one in Florida. She has twenty-one grandchildren and one great-grandchild.

Her writings have recently brought her honors and recognition. In March of 1974, Voorhees College invited her to address the students and awarded her a certificate of achievement. She was invited to address the Columbia Writers' Club in 1972, and since then has traveled extensively in connection with her career as a writer. Of particular importance to her has been her friendship with Dr. Everetta Love Blair, the author of *Jessie Stuart: His Life and Works*. But Mrs. Nelson denies any influence on her works of any literary figure: "I've always wanted to be me," she says. "I didn't want to copy anything or anybody."

Mrs. Nelson's books everywhere reflect the Christianity that has been and continues to be such an important part of her life. Brought up to observe regular prayer and Bible reading, she considers Christianity the foundation of her existence. She observes the events of the present in the light of her religion: "Unless we have a spiritual awakening, unless people go back to God," she says, "I think we are doomed."

Nevertheless Mrs. Nelson sees the present and future as an opportunity for men and women of both races to make a contribution to history. Particularly for blacks does she view the necessity for forgetting, forgiving, and building bridges. "It's our job to help provide the love, patience, and understanding necessary to get things done."

Mrs. Nelson's own life is an exemplum of the courage, determination, and hope necessary to realize an amibition in the face of obstacles and lack of opportunity. The titles of her books reflect her own progress from storm to calm, from darkness to light. She summed it up well in her own statement of hope and accomplishment—"Don't walk on my dreams!"

Margaret C. Thomas
The Reprint Company, Publishers

May 1976
Spartanburg, S.C.

Don't Walk on My Dreams

By
Annie Green Nelson

Published by the Author
2129½ Oak Street
Columbia, South Carolina

Illustrations by the Messrs. Edward L. Nelson and Fred Pettiway.

Preface

Last summer, I took a trip into the Southland, 'way down in South Carolina. At least to me, a northerner, South Carolina is 'way down! A certain propelling destiny guided me there, a destiny both human and divine. I did want to visit the land of my forefathers some day, not suspecting that it would be under such circumstances.

One enjoyable experience came out of that trip: I met the author of Don't Walk on My Dreams, a tender and warm-hearted story of southern Negro folk at home. I had the privilege of hearing this and many other human interest stories from the lips of Mrs. Annie Green Nelson. She is well-versed in southern Negro folklore, having lived it and having loved the people of whom she writes. This story is the heart and soul of the author crying out in the wilderness of the southern plantation scene of her story of the American Negro in the perspective of American history.

The characterization of these fascinating figures of American life reveal an intimate knowledge of the inner life of the American Negro. All you have to do is look into your own community. They are there, all around you. They have been there since America was America. They are a part of her and she is a part of them.

The main players on the stage of the story of the American Negro in the Southland were the teacher and the preacher. Their many problems and heartaches are depicted in the lives of Reb Eli and Sugar

Babe, and in the accomplishments of Bill as teacher and then principal of the Warrenville school. These brought their education back to their people and lifted them above established norms. These educators became recognized as leaders by the white community and by their own people.

Granny Jenny could be your own grandmother. And in your family, you might find an Aunt Molly. Perhaps, they would not be exactly the same, but the basic character of old folks at home is there. The good, old common sense, the hard sense, that came from a life of toil and subservience has shaped their lives and their dreams. They are lovable people, nevertheless; they are the backbone of family life.

The religious life of the southern Negro is a mainstay of southern Negro folklore. Who can but feel a tear or inner tug at the heart for Uncle Friday, asking God to come to his relief! It is the longing cry of a lost soul seeking a way out of the lifelong hardships of the Negro.

And, of course, there are Paw Vest and Maw Vest. What a life it was for them to bring up their family through it all! There are other familiar people in this story. I am sure you will find one that you know. And let us thank Annie Green Nelson for this opportunity to relive with her one of the most remarkable stories that can be told about the history of the American Negro and his contributions to the life of the South.

Let us leave them all—Paw and Maw Vest, Reb Eli, Sugar Babe, Bill, Uncle Friday, Aunt Molly and the others—with the idea that the things which they have given are the gifts of a noble people, for only a people who are noble indeed could give so much and receive so little.

SYDNEY H. GALLWEY

Ithaca, N. Y., November 1, 1961.

Contents

Illustrations

CHAPTER I

Plantation Days

THE hot summer sun had gone down and Granny Jenny had moved her chair out under the old oak tree where she could enjoy the shady, pleasant breeze. She heard the sound of a buggy crossing the old wooden bridge. "Bet dat Rev. Eli. He usually come around to see about me when I miss church, and I jest didn't feel a bit like being dere last Sunday," Granny mused to herself as the sound came nearer.

Soon a buggy came in sight. Granny Jenny called: "Cum here, Sugar Babe! Dat der preacher man is coming down dat road; run, sweep off de front porch and git another cheer 'cause your pappy'll be home toreckly, and fetch some cool water from de pump. Put it in dat big, white pitcher in the company room. 'Spect Reb. Eli gwine spend der night. He done come sich a fur ways."

Sugar Babe soon had the porch swept and water in the pitcher in the company room. "See bout dem biscuits in de stove, run to der coop and fetch one of dem fryers for his supper. You know how he love chicken."

Granny Jenny began getting up to meet the Reverend Eli. "Show is the gladdest in der world to see you," she told him as he reached for her hand.

1

Sunny and Bun soon finished feeding the mules and horses and were met at the door by Granny Jenny whispering: "Be quiet, der preacher is here and wash der dust off your faces and walk easy so you can't 'terb him."

They were accustomed to that type of behavior around grownups and especially when the Reverend Eli came or Miss Henrietta, the adored school m'am.

"Here come Maw," Sugar Babe said, looking out the side window toward the big house where her mother Lou cooked. Yes, every day some nice surprise awaited them in the big dishpan Maw brought from Lem's house.

After the Rev. Eli ate, he and Paw Vest went out on the porch to talk about some church matter, Paw Vest being one of the deacons. Maw took this opportunity to instruct the children in the proper use of words. She would have them repeat after her this, that, those and all the "big words" she had heard the Lems' children using. Maw's children were considered the most intelligent children in that community for Paw Vest and Maw Lou had always worked around "the house," thus acquiring much of the Lems' culture.

When Sugar Babe was very small, they had her singing like Anna Lems, who was taking voice. Paw being the official music teacher on the plantation, every Tuesday night taught singing lessons in the big sitting room. All his nine children could and did sing. Sugar Babe led all the songs at the little one-teacher school that sat 'way back in the corner of the woods. She had the leading parts in all the plays.

One day when Maw and Paw were in the field with their nine children, Paw Vest said, "Lou, this is a good time to ask these younguns what they are going to be when they grow up. Let us start asking Sugar Babe." No sooner than Paw had asked the question, Sugar Babe informed him she was going to be a teacher. Maw's big, brown face lit up like a lamp while Paw smiled and looked on with pride, for to them Miss Henrietta was like an angel sent from Heaven to direct their way. Sugar Babe even tried to walk like her. Of course, Sunny and Bun said they were going to be farmers, while Jacob, one of the twins, said he was going to be a preacher like Rev. Eli, and urged Maw to buy him a Bible for Christmas.

Sunday came, and the Rev. Eli had prayer with the family and left for church. He took the twins, Esaw and Jacob, with him. It was revival time and a great crowd was expected. One side of the church had been reserved for "white folks" who always attended the revival in large numbers and contributed largely toward its support. At the end of the week there were a large number of converts, among them Big Hannah who weighed nearly three hundred pounds. She was married to "Little Slim" whom she spanked any time she considered he needed it. There were many happy mothers and fathers, husbands and wives rejoicing over conversion of their loved ones, but "Little Slim" was happiest of all.

After the revival, the Rev. Eli went back to Maw Lou's to collect his week's gifts given him by the members during his stay among them. When he arrived, Granny Jenny met him at the door in her pretty, clean, white apron. "Come in, Reb—herd you done some coal burning in dis hear vival. Show wish I coulda been dere, but I keep so poorly lately. I don't git anywhere 'cepting up at der 'big house' to see my chillin. You know I help raise dem Lems so I old now and dey seem to feel 'sponsible fur all dese

3

negroes on his place. Most of dem been here all dey life so dey kinda look to him fur everything. He taught them everything.''

Just as Granny Jenny, who was Sis Lou's mother, stopped talking, supper was announced by Paw Vest. After the Rev. Eli had washed his hands in the wash basin in the company room and started out to look for a towel on the rack in the kitchen, Granny Jenny said, "Reb, here jest wipe your hands dry on this here apron. It's clean. I just put it on." The Rev. Eli dried his hands, trying to hold back a laugh that got away as soon as he was seated at the table and told his customary joke. Sis Lou could hardly hold her head up when she found out what Granny Jenny had done. She could hardly wait to give Sugar Babe a raking out for not having a clean towel in the "company room." Next morning, the Rev. Eli left.

After all, he always enjoyed these simple farm folks; they were so kind and sincere. In their way, they went all out to make one happy. The Rev. Eli thought as he rode back to Warrensville that they truly practice the saying, "Love thy neighbor." He had learned something from them in each of his visits. He remembered that when Sugar Babe was very small, he had visited them on a Saturday in the winter. When he got there, Sugar Babe had three potatoes in the fire, covered with ashes. He was hungry, and while he waited for dinner, began eating Sugar Babe's potatoes as she looked on. After he had eaten two, Sugar Babe thought he would eat the others. She jumped out of the corner of the fireplace, ran over to him and said, "Look here, Eli, don't eat all my tatoes." He often laughed about that.

Fall came and the crops were being gathered. All sang as they worked in adjoining fields. Paw

4

Vest was stacking and racking hay. Sugar Babe, who was growing to be a pretty young miss, wanted to help Paw stack hay. Sunny and Bun were helping Mernera, Helen, Evelyn and Nita with the cotton and fodder pulling. Sugar Babe, being the eldest girl and a favorite of Paw's, usually got what she wanted. So Paw let her get up on the haystack and stack hay like a man, but there was nothing mannish about this pretty, brown girl, and that could readily be seen by the attention she was getting from the menfolk who happened to pass during the day.

Bost, the young and handsome son of the Rev. O'Keep, could not resist the temptation and stopped by as Sugar Babe was capping the last stack of hay. She looked down at him, smiling with those big brown eyes that twinkled like the stars when she laughed.

"You look mighty pretty up there stacking hay. Don't you know that's a man's job?" Bost said. "Oh! but I don't only help Paw stack the hay; I plow, too, sometimes. I love it."

Jokingly, Bost said: "Well, you are the kind of a girl I would like for a wife." Then he got off his horse and, as she slid down the haystack, he caught her in his arms. Sugar Babe had never had an experience like that so, as they walked home together from the field, she thought for the first time "how wonderful it must be to be in love."

When Sis Lou saw her daughter walking with Bost, she began to scold Paw for leaving her alone in the field to finish stacking the hay. "You know these boys around here, and you know Sugar Babe is young and she ain't got much sense, so you have to watch after her. She is just sixteen." Sis Lou had forgotten that she had run away and married Paw when

5

she was only sixteen. When she began to scold Sugar Babe about walking home with Bost, Sugar Babe reminded her of her early marriage. Although Sis Lou called her "sassy," she had to admist the truth herself.

Time passed swiftly. The year's work was finished. People on the plantation had heard about the war. Paw, who was in his forties, thought he would like to volunteer, but Mr. Lems advised him to stay with the farm. "Vest, we need food and clothes for the war, so don't think you aren't helping out because you are not on the battlefield. You have an important part to play here and you are doing a good job of it." Paw went home and told Maw Lou what Mr. Lems said. "That suits me fine 'cause I dunno what I would do without you now with all these children to care for. Too, Sugar Babe graduates in June, and Miss Henrietta thinks we should send her to college. She and Alice Smith will be the first children to graduate from this here school."

Paw Vest would be the proudest man on the plantation. He would have a daughter in college, he thought, as he worked day after day, trying to adjust himself to the changing plantation scenes.

On April 7 of that year, the United States declared war on Germany. All the boys who were old enough to answer the call had to go. Most of them had never been farther away than the little town of Warrenville and they had little education, if any. The majority was attached to the 371st Division but they didn't have time to do much military training before they were on their way to France to help stop the "Huns" or the Kaiser. Many of these boys marched off the plantation never to return. They gave their lives that we might enjoy the freedom they could never know. Some of those who returned were restless. They no more could be satisfied to retire to a life of hoeing and plowing, the life in which they once found happiness. They had been to France.

They heard of a better world; they hoped, they dreamed and planned to enter it as soon as they returned. "How are you going to keep 'em down on the farm" was a reality. Mr. Lems tried, with others, to discourage his Negroes from going North. It was no use. They had had a taste of a better life than anything they thought they had ever known. The "North" found itself with a problem. Did the Negroes find the freedom there they sought? Had they ever lived so poorly as a whole on the southern plantations? Did anyone seem really to care for these creatures, many of whom could neither read nor write? Many could not name a town in France; all they knew was, they had been to France. Some returned to the plantation, some stayed. Northern cold weather took its toll of many who were not properly clothed and fed during the winter.

The oldsters mostly stuck to their guns and would not budge. Paw Vest said, "I have always lived in these parts and now I am too old to break up and leave, too. I get along all right, me and my children." He expressed the sentiment of lots of those who had stuck their roots deep in the old South and were not being deceived by fantastic stories about the North. One day Paw Vest and his wife were discussing the situation. "You know, Lou, the white folks here have been looking after us all our lives. I think it's about time for me and my family to try to stand on our own feet. I believe I'll buy a little home with the little 'nest eggs' I got in the bank. You see, Sugar Babe is in college now and she would love a place to call her

7

own when she brings her college friends around."

"I sure am in for that," Maw Lou said, "but what about us leaving the Lems? We been here all us life; wonder what will he say."

When the end of that year came and Paw settled his account with Mr. Lems, he explained his plans and to his surprise Mr. Lems seemed pleased, as bad as he said he hated to see them leave.

Granny Jenny was their problem. She thought she could never leave her "chillin," as she called the Lems. "Dunno what I'll do if you take me 'way frum here, us born and raise here. Now, you gwine leave; you must be crazy. I ain't gwine nowhare. Dere's a little house in the yard and I gwine ask to stay dare and do what little I kin around her house. Why I nurse Bill Lems' daddy, and I know dey ain't gwine turn me down."

So up to the "big house" she went, and when Paw Vest moved into his own little five-room house surrounded by the forty acres of land he bought, Granny Jenny moved into her little house in the Lems' back yard. There she could dream and live in a past, a beautiful past she could never forget.

" 'Niggers' never got restless around here until they went to war," Mr. McCloud said to Mr. Lems one day while visiting, and Maw Lou, who was still cooking for the Lems, overhead him. Mr. Lems just shook his head as Mr. McCloud went on: "We gotta do something to bring them back in line. I ain't got enough help to gather my crop. All pulling up going 'north.' That boy of old George who went to France is plum biggety since he got back. Why yestidy he give me some sass, and I be d—— if I am going to take that off any 'nigger.' "

Jim had just returned and was employed at Mr.

8

McCloud's gin. Of course, the Negroes on Mr. Lems' place never ventured over the creek on McCloud's place; it was a known fact that he hated "niggers." So when he jumped on Jim the next day to whip him, it was no surprise. When the battle was over, Mr. McCloud had to be taken home and put to bed, from which he swore vengeance. Some of the wiser and kinder whites advised Jim to get as far away as possible and do so as quickly as he could.

CHAPTER II

Change Comes to the Old Plantation

BOST, who was now in love with Sugar Babe, was one of the young people whose heart was entwined around Lems' plantation. He had come back and begun to save money so he could get married. begun to save his money so he could get married. When Maw heard it, she said: "No, what does he think I am educating my daughter to be a teacher like Miss Henrietta for. To marry some ignorant farming man. No! a thousand times no!"

However, he and Sugar Babe, whose real name was Eve, continued exchanging love letters while they were apart. He would plow and dream and plan their future. He remembered the first word he ever said to her. It was at her Aunt Pearl's wedding. She was so pretty, he thought, in her little lace and rose-colored frilled dress. He thought she looked like a doll with her hair in ringlets, her twinkling, bright eyes that seemed to flash a bright light when she laughed. While they were being served at the wedding, Eve asked him about a girl she had seen him with. His reply was: "If I tell you who I am in love with, you'd be surprised." With a quick, devilish little laugh that curved her pretty pink mouth, she asked, "Who?" ""You," Bost answered with a serious look on his handsome face. It was just what this little sixteen-year-old girl was wishing he would say, and he did.

Now, she had finished the little tenth grade school at Warrenville, after leaving the one-room schoolhouse in the corner of the woods where the children of the plantations were stuffed in like sardines. Eve had been among the group who carried chitlings, hog cracklings, pone bread, peas and potatoes to school in their large tin buckets. She had waved them around the room at noontime for the children to claim their dinner. She had sat with her friends waiting her turn to get to chew the piece of gum some one of the group had brought to school.

Now, Eve was in college where she had acquired the culture and dignity of those who were privileged to attend a school of higher learning. So Maw Lou would see to it that she didn't marry Bost, a plantation hand, as she called him.

Granny Jenny was no better for she was so glad to see Eve graduate that she jumped up out of her seat when the teacher presented the certificate. Granny hollered, "Uh-uh, to see dat gal educating makes me get up off it!" That was the first time Granny Jenny and many others on the plantation had ever seen a graduation.

Paw Vest, having become a landowner, came to be recognized among his people as a "big dog." They elected him chairman of the Negro Trustee Board, a deacon in the church and leader of the choir. As he began to improve his lot by getting out on his own, he began to give short talks to his people about being thrifty. "You just as well learn to stand on your own feet. Someday Mr. Lems is going to get tired carrying you around on his back year after year. Send your children to school. This war has proven the need for an education. What can a man do that can't read and write but dig ditches and shovel all his life. Let's get together and work toward better school facilities here," Paw Vest told

11

them, and by the end of the year a Rosenwald school was replacing the little one-room schoolhouse. All didn't agree, but Paw Vest, who had the advantage of finishing the Warrenville graded school and studying music, too, could always muster enough help to put over any community project he thought needed.

He and Maw Lou were loved by both races and had their respect. They continued to help out at the big house on such occasions as Christmas, New Year's and Thanksgiving. They loved the Lems' plantation and would always remember the happy days spent there but, as Paw said, "A man ought to learn to walk alone sometime, especially if he expects to enjoy what the other people enjoy; and, too, if he wants respect, he's got to get himself in a respectable position."

College had closed for summer vacation and Eve was home again. Maw Lou let her know in no uncertain tone that she wasn't going to have her going around with Bost. "Don't the Bible say 'Be not unequally yoked together'?" So Maw Lou set nine o'clock as a deadline for bedtime, and whenever Bost or any other boy friend came, Maw Lou would sit outside the door watching the clock. When nine o'clock came, with a big stick she would knock on the wall of the old-time parlor nine times, and Eve would get up and get the young man's hat in order to avoid further embarrassment. Kissing him goodnight was out of the question for, if Maw wasn't at the door, Paw Vest was standing outside the window. So Eve grew up and finished college before she had ever been kissed.

Strange as it may seem, Paw Vest and Maw Lou acted like love was a deadly poison always to be

12

avoided by their children. They gave them all the necessities for life, they thought.

Mernera, who was the most quiet girl of the Greene family, thought out a plan to help Eve so that her company could stay longer. One day when Eve said to her, "Look like it took nine o'clock longer to come last night than usual," Mernera laughed to herself. She was afraid to trust her secret to anyone for she knew that if Maw Lou ever found out, one of the old-time punishments would be given her. Maw Lou didn't believe in beating on clothes, as she would say. Hence, it was the year Eve was graduating before she learned from Mernera that she had been turning the hands on the clock back an hour.

September came too soon, and again Eve left for college. One morning she woke up frightened. She had had the saddest dream about Paw Vest. She dreamed he was dead, and she was standing over the grave, crying. While eating dinner that day she was called to the President's office where she found a telegram saying, "Come at once." She arrived home in time enough to spend one night with Paw Vest. He grew steadily worse.

The old rooster looked away from the house and crowed. The spider web moved lower on the wall. The tears dropped out of Maw Lou's eyes in Paw Vest's face as he reached and took her hand and bade farewell to the troubles of this old world. Around his bedside stood the doctor, Eve, Sunny, Jake and Evelyn. He had asked Maw to pull the pillow from under his head. Then he looked at Evelyn and said, "I want to be looking over the battlements of glory and seeing you children obeying your Maw."

Sunny, who had been in the war and who seemed

13

so strong, held Paw's hands as the teardrops told the story of his deep grief.

When Mr. Lems heard the news, he lost no time in getting to Paw's bedside, and cried when he found that he was too late. Paw had gone to join those who had passed before. Mr. Lems asked Maw Lou, "Is

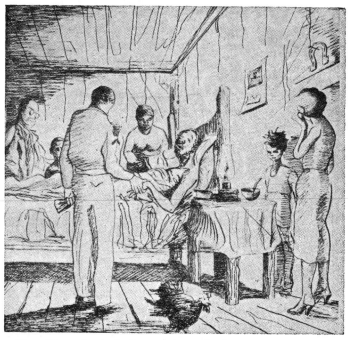

The old rooster looked away from the house and crowed. The spider web moved lower on the wall. The tears dropped out of Maw Lou's eyes into Paw Vest's face. All looked on as Paw bid farewell to the trouble of this old world.

there anything I can do?" Maw Lou was too shaken and shocked to answer. She nodded her head in the negative.

"Vest Greene is sure going to be missed," Mr. Lems

14

told some of the field hands that day, when they inquired about his condition after seeing Mr. Lems leave the house.

Yes, Vest Greene, with his ready wit, plain philosophy of living and his kindness to the poor around him would surely be missed. They had seen him on weekends fill his wagon with food and distribute it around in the community where there was need. Sometimes Maw Lou would scold and say, "Vest, those people are just plain lazy. They don't even plant a garden. They won't even try. Why bother?" Vest would smile and say he was just carrying out his own conviction of "love thy neighbor." Then on Sundays, after attending church, he would walk miles to teach a Sunday school class at Lunn siding, an isolated section of the country without a church. He would laugh and say he believed he had been called to preach. "I just walk behind the plow and preach all day," he told Maw Lou one day. "Must be God wanting me to go preach his word." Maw thought so too, but decided to let Paw Vest reach his own decision.

After Paw's death, Granny Jenny came to live with Maw Lou, her daughter. "Thought you'd be lonesome without me since Vest done died," Granny said as she came in the front door where her daughter was ironing clothes for the children. "I thought you were Sugar Babe," Maw Lou said, looking up into the dusty, wrinkled face of her mother.

"Sure glad you come. It all seemed like a dream. I can't believe Vest is gone. I keep looking for him to come in or listen to hear him laugh and tell a joke like he told about his hair." There was a smile on Maw Lou's face now. When Granny interrupted, "What was hit? I know it was a 'case' if Vest told it." Now, Maw Lou was laughing as she began, "You know Vest used to say when teased about his red, knotty hair, 'The only way my hair will look like it's combed when I go to church is for me to stand on the top steps and comb it, then jump in the church door!' " They both had a hearty laugh which helped dispel some of the gloom that had settled over that home.

"Sugar Babe will leave tomorrow for college. You know she will graduate in June," Maw Lou finished. She was thinking of all the plans Paw Vest had for Babe and then, right near the end of his struggle to get her through college, he died.

Granny reminded Maw, "Yes, she is taking Vest's death mighta hard. You know she was her pappy's heart."

Maw Lou didn't hear Granny Jenny's last words. She was deep in thoughts. "What am I going to do. Sunny will have to take over the farm. No more school for him." The thoughts of his not being able to finish school hurt her most of all; then, the doctor told her to go away for a while because, "If you don't, you will be a nervous wreck," Dr. Sims had said.

Because Maw Lou didn't know anything about business, Mr. Lems came over and helped her get her insurance and told her how to plan and carry on the farm. Yet, although Maw Lou and Paw Vest had moved away on their own land, they still felt a part of the old plantation on which they, their parents and grandparents had always lived. All of them had "laid down the shovel and hoe," except Granny Jenny, and had left the old "camping ground" in order to join the "great camp meeting in the Promised Land."

16

When Sugar Babe graduated, Mrs. Lems made her a white voile dress. "Yes, she is the first colored girl to graduate from this section and we are all proud of her," she told her neighbors. Everybody made much ado over her but Granny Jenny sensed a little change in Sugar Babe. "Now, us proud of yur, but don't let dis learning swell your head. Yur Pappy and Mammy worked awful hard to send you to school. Remember dat and tank der Lurd you had betta chance dan de outhers round here. Show yur 'preciation by trying to help outhers lack your Pappy use to do.

"Right now I need yur to put some water in de wash pot. I gwine help Lou do de washing and I want you to take dem overhauls I got soaking in kerosene what dem boys done got filthy down in der ditch digging it out, and paddle der dirt out of dem on dat old paddling block."

Sugar Babe hummed and did her chores and prepared to go out to the club meeting that she had organized at Shady Grove. It was the first club ever to be organized in that church, and she called it "The Young Women's Development Club." It was such a success that it attracted quite a number of middle-aged women of the community who joined in and worked earnestly with the girls. They got as great a thrill out of it as the girls did, especially the social side. They appeared with the young people on many of their programs and thus added interest to the work of the young people in Shady Grove Church and community.

Sugar Babe was not happy because she had a college education that made her long for something else besides the things she had on the old plantation. She longed to see more of the world about which she had studied; hence, she begged Maw Lou to let her

17

go with some friends to Battle Creek, Michigan. What a thrill to be leaving the old plantation for such a long trip through Kentucky, Ohio, Indiana and finally arriving in Kalamazoo early on a bright Sunday morning. She would never forget the mountainous scenes of North Carolina, nor the beautiful green valleys of Kentucky and Indiana. She often expressed it as a place where everything you see looks good to you.

Maw Lou was sorry she wanted to leave home, but convinced herself that Sugar Babe was right by saying to her inquiring neighbors, "You can't keep 'em tied to your apron string all the time. They're like the little birds when they grow big enough, they leave the nest."

Granny Jenny didn't like Maw Lou's explanation and expressed her own feeling about it. "Lou, Sugar Babe ain't no bird and can't fly high 'nough to get out dey way of de temptations she gwine meet up da road, and you'll see. When I was raising you chillin when we thought a thing wasn't good for you, me and your Pappy said no and meant no, and you chillin knowed bettern question why us said no. Now, you let dese younguns argue you down and make you give in, den you blame dem fur misbehaving. Dey ain't to blame. Hit's you, Lou. Dat gal never shoulda been 'loud to go up dat road tu work. Ain't you educated her tu teach?"

Time passed and Maw Lou saw the wisdom in Granny's position. Although Sugar Babe had gotten work, she was homesick and wanted to return to the old plantation and to those she loved. Nevertheless, Maw Lou determined to make her stick out a year, since many of the neighbors had said she wouldn't stay long.

18

When Maw Lou advised her to stay, Sugar Babe read the letter and fell across her roommate's bed and boohooed. "Of course, I want to work and help Maw with the other children, but the people here are so different from what I heard and expected. Just think, this morning on my way to work I sat beside a white lady and she turned her back to me. I much rather be home where the people are friendly, if they like you, and, too, I know what to expect and am not embarrassed by sitting beside someone who resents me." "Oh, what do you care about that," was the reply of Kay, Sugar Babe's roommate. "Come, go to the show tonight with me and Bob, my boy friend."

It was at the Bijou and there were two comedians who came out singing "Are You from Dixie?" As each would ask the other "Are you from Dixie?" they met in the center of the stage and shook hands and exclaimed, "Yes, I am from Dixie too." In the middle of the left aisle was a brown-skinned girl standing and weeping softly. No one knew the reason why everybody stared. Then suddenly she realized everybody was looking at her. She sat down quietly. 'Way down deep in her soul, she was singing, "Yes, I am from Dixie, too."

Sugar Babe was surely the "lonesomest gal in town." She was standing there seeing the old plantation house with its big, wide, shady porch and yard; the old quilting frames that Maw Lou kept tucked up in the rafters of the back porch; the big, old paddling block that Paw Vest had sawed for Maw when they were all small; that little black wash pot where all their children's clothes were boiled with lye and rinsed until they were snowy

19

white. She had a vision of the old clothes line, the little privy that Maw Lou had them keep scrubbed and "clean as a pin" in which all the stove ashes were poured; and, most of all, she missed the plantation hands singing as they worked.

Maw Lou had to keep busy to make ends meet so she sent Granny Jenny to New York to spend a while with her younger sister, who had come down for her. "Now, Mamma sings everywhere she go, Liz," Maw Lou said as she began packing Granny Jenny's clothes. "If she isn't singing out, she hums. You can't make her take her headrag off, either. She says her head is cold." Liz thought a while and replied, "You know I am not going to stand for that."

However, Liz didn't know Granny. She didn't realize that Granny, although aged, had not lost one bit of the stubbornness she possessed when young— if she felt she was right. She lumbered up to the "Big House" to tell Mr. Lems and his family goodby, for it was the first time she had left the community. "Hum, dey dragging me up dat road in my old age lack I can't take care muself while Lou work. Must think I crazy since I got ole. Lou talk about I may catch fire. Whut does she think I is?" Granny grumbled to herself as she moved toward Mr. Lems. "Jest come to say goodby; you know I ole now and may not git back but couldn't go widout seeing my chillin." Mrs. Lems went back into the house and, when she came out, she brought a package for Granny to take with her. "Musta knowed I needed a nice frock and some long drawers," Granny said to her daughter, as she cried and laughed at the same time.

Mr. Lems and Mrs. Lems were going to miss "Aunt

20

Jenny," as they called her. "You know ever since the war, after all the boys went to the Army and come back, nothing has seemed the same around the plantation. Looks like I have sensed a feeling of unrest among the Negroes. It's only the old ones that stick. Most of the young ones leave as soon as they get old enough. Well, I guess they are like any other people, change according to circumstances, and we have to accept it," Mrs. Lems said after some thought. "Mark my word," Mr. Lems said, "Aunt Jenny will never stay with Liz in New York."

The year had passed and Sugar Babe had come back home to stay but, as Granny had said, she was a gal and not a bird and couldn't fly high enough to avoid temptation. Sugar Babe had fallen in love and found out too late that it was a one-sided affair. Heartbroken, she returned home to find Bost married to her best girl friend. "Yes, he had married her best girl friend a week ago," her sister Mernera said as Sugar Babe got off the train and was en route to the old plantation. She felt as if she had just experienced a double tragedy. Was it? No, out of her experiences were to come an inspired, lovelier womanhood; an aim and desire to render service to humanity. She was crestfallen yet, deep down inside, she vowed, "No one will ever know the truth about me. No one will ever know how much it hurts."

Granny Jenny was in New York, acting like a fish out of water. She refused to walk up the five flights of stairs to Liz's apartment. Each time they went out and came back she insisted on taking off her shoes and crawling up the steps. When Liz hung out the clothes, she refused to let her long drawers hang " 'way up da twixt heaven and earth for everybody

21

to see." Hence, Liz had to dry them in the kitchen on a chair.

Then Granny just wouldn't stop singing. "Maw, you just got to stop singing tomorrow 'cause I got to go down town to Times Square and I can't leave you up here, so you can't sing even if it's low in tone." "What did she say that for? What do you mean, I can't sing?" Granny asked. Teasingly Liz replied, "You aren't down South. You are in 'Yankee Land' " Her dander up, the aged lady responded to this by throwing off her old, black jacket and coming out fighting. "Yankee Land or no Yankee Land, I gwine sing fur mur Jesus." Sure enough she made good her promise. On the train downtown she hummed, "Do you think I will ever make a soldier?" Everybody was watching her, but she was looking straight ahead with her old, starched red kerchief on her head and a kindly, tender look on her dusty, wrinkled, worn face and a brilliant light of faith in her eyes as she sat there and sang for her Jesus.

She didn't recognize or even care about the embarrassment Liz was suffering while looking out of the window and trying to appear to be a stranger. When they got off at the downtown station, Liz almost threatened her mother about humming a song on the train. Did that stop her? No! While Liz was shopping in a crowded section, the old lady moved slowly along singing. Then suddenly a policeman came along and told her to "Move on." "Move on whar? You must live in Yankee Land," she said. Just as the officer was about to book her and take her to a hospital for examination, Liz came on the scene and began to explain. A photographer nearby took her picture and she was interviewed. "Yes, I allus sing. I got something inside dat sings hits. My soul dats happy, dats all." The next day there appeared in one of the leading papers a story about the little, old lady with a song in her heart who dared to sing in "Yankee Land"—on Times Square.

Sugar Babe was teaching now and Maw Lou had stopped cooking for the Lems. Sunny and Bun, Evelyn and Helen and Mernera and Juanita were helping Maw Lou with the gathering of the crops. Maw had said she would do the cooking but found it so lonesome at home "without Vest until I had rather help in the field."

One evening, as the children stopped work Maw went home alone. As she turned the bend around the pines, she screamed at the top of her voice a frightful scream. All the children went running to her rescue. When she recovered well enough to tell what had happened, she said that when she reached the bend there was Paw waiting for her, and as she got near, he gave a long, tired sigh. After that Paw was often seen by one of the children either out in the barn feeding the cattle or chickens or in the yard.

Sugar Babe advised Maw to sell the house and move to town. "There the children will have better advantages for school," she said. To this Maw agreed and that was the worst bargain Maw Lou had ever made. Maw Lou belonged to the old plantation because some of the children were still growing and needed the wide-open space. Maw Lou was not accustomed to cramped quarters. She knew her neighbors and they knew her. She loved her neighbors and they loved her.

CHAPTER III

Sugar Babe Faces Life

GRANNY Jenny told Liz, "I 'um plum sicka dis here place. I wan to go back to Mr. Lems'. Da I wanta live and die." Liz arranged to take her mother back to the old South that Granny loved so much; the plantation where she had roamed as a child, where she felt free to sing wherever she chanced to go, and where nobody questioned her folkways and lores. On the way South, Granny Jenny sang, "Wait till my feet strike Zion, won't I be glad." Liz never tried to stop her as she sat humming but was glad when she talked or slept.

Everybody was glad to see Granny. She moved into her own little house in the Lems' back yard where she could reach the kitchen easily from the side door. Every day, as had been her custom, she went over to the "big house" to help around, as she called it. Mrs. Lems allowed her to help and instructed the other help not to meddle with her.

"I was de gladest to get back here tu my chillin," she said as she put her arms around Mrs. Lems' shoulders. Yes, the Lems were her chillin. She said, "I nursed Jimmy Lems' daddy and I nursed Jimmy. Now, I ole and jest hang around, but they see after me."

One morning in the spring, Granny didn't come in

24

for her breakfast. No one had heard her singing all morning. Mrs. Lems sent the cook over with some food to see if she was sick. There, in a chair by the fireplace she sat fully clothed, hands folded, a faint smile on her face as if she had said, "I just crossed over." Her songs had ended, and she had gathered up her spiritual belongings and had boarded the "Old Ship of Zion." There she joined the angelic host in songs and praises to Him who is King of Kings, and Lord of Lords.

Mr. Lems' family and all the plantation hands were at the funeral. Her life had been an open book of inspiration to all who knew her.

Maw Lou and children rented a farm. Maw found it hard to support the children without a farm.

Sugar Babe was going to be married to one of the boys who had served overseas. She was marrying Bill Brown. Down in her heart she knew she didn't love him, but was determined to make it stick. After all, he was a fine young man and ambitious, too. He had finished school in New York and, when he came to Warrenville to teach, everyone welcomed "their" Bill. "These are the common grounds on which we can build," she thought.

Time passed and Sugar Babe found it hard living with a man she didn't love. She felt a sense of guilt in accepting all the nice things he did and gave. Finally, she learned that she was to become a mother, and hoped that this would bridge the gap. She asked herself this question, "Can a baby bring love into the heart of a woman for a man whom she does not love?" She knew the answer, but wouldn't admit it. Yet long ago she had given her heart away. There she had built a world of beauty, a world to call her own. In it were no clouds or shadows. She loved Bob

25

and him alone. Yes, he had left her sad and yearning, yearning for him each day. Now, she could not find the answer. Neither could she find a way. For the world she built had vanished, vanished with love's setting sun. Although she dared not admit it, she thought Bob would always be the only one.

Sugar Babe continued to teach. After the baby was a year old, Maw Lou noticed how strange Sugar Babe acted and called her in for a conference.

"Listen, I notice when Little Ruth called you yesterday, you didn't answer until she had called Mrs. Eve three times. What's on your mind?" It looked as if it was just what Eve was waiting for, for the first time since her father's death she put her head on Maw Lou's lap and cried like a little girl who had lost her only doll.

Maw Lou was a woman of understanding. She called it good "horse sense" and she told her about the fundamentals on which love is built: "Respect, appreciation of all the good in a body," she said. "Don't close yourself into a selfish shell and refuse to budge. Give a little, take a little and don't look for perfection in Bill. What if he knew how you felt about him. You can't, you must not for your own self and the baby's. Let him know you all need each other so much. Build your home on the solid rock Christ Jesus and you will soon find yourself like Paul 'forgetting the things which are behind'."

Sugar Babe promised to give Maw's formula a trial, and by the end of that year she told Maw: "I have a heart that is true. I feel no more guilt but we are one happy family, living, loving and sharing."

Mr. Lems' wife became very sick. Someone had to stay with her, so Mr. Lems drove to Warrenville to ask Maw Lou to come and help out by nursing Mrs.

Lems. "We don't have Aunt Jenny any more so we come for you. Lou, she doesn't want anybody else to nurse her. She is like she was when Tom was born and Docter Kitt said she was too run down to nurse him. I tried to get somebody but she refused to have anybody nurse Tom but you, Lou, and I think we brought him to you on a pillow, weighing four pounds and in six weeks he was gaining. We could handle him without a pillow. He is employed by the State now; got a big job, weighs two hundred pounds or more."

Maw Lou with her brown face and high cheeks had a queer little smile that curved her lips. "Yes, since he growed up and got to be a man he forgot me, but I nursed him right along with my Sugar Babe, and he still belong to me." Mr. Lems laughed and said, "Lou, we aren't never going to forget you. Come on. Reckon Mrs. Lems' looking for you. She said she would feel better if you came."

Maw Lou moved in to wait on Mrs. Lems who grew steadily worse. Standing with the family at the funeral was Maw Lou, weeping her heart out. She had lost one of the best friends she ever knew.

After the death of Mrs. Lems the old plantation lost much of its charm. All of Mr. Lems' children had left home. There were no more hog-killing days when all met and shared this annual time together. Mr. Lems moved to town and rented out the farm. Most of the older Negroes, like their children, went different directions, seeking kinder shepherds than those folk who rented the farm; anyone who had ever lived in that community could readily see that with the passing of the farm out of Mr. Lems' hands, the end of an era had come.

Now, Maw Lou just didn't know how she would

be able to get along without them for she had a "backbone," as she called it, as long as the Lems lived. Then she remembered what Paw Vest had told them after the war. "The time is coming when the Negro has to stand on his own two feet. The whites will get tired of toting him when he begins to make so many demands, and when a people become educated, they begin to search and think in doing that. They begin reaching for everything the other fellow enjoys."

Paw had worked to improve the school building. He was the first to send his daughter to college from that community. He was looking away into the future. He often asked his audience, did the Negro have any standard for which he would die? Does he have a heritage? Then he would say, "until we are trained well enough to participate fully, we will always have to take the back seat in American life. We gotta train our people; we gotta love our people. Try to own something besides the pants you got on your backs." He always ended by getting a hearty applause from the audience.

Sugar Babe, or Little Eve as she was called by some, was still carrying her father's training. "Be the best of whatever you are," he would say. He meant it for he made his children do a job until it was perfect, even when cutting and piling wood.

The years went by, and Mernera became a teacher, Evelyn became a writer, Helen became an actress; Jacob, one of the twins, became a preacher, Sunny and Bun stuck to the farm, but now they own the big plantation that they worked. On Sunny's farm were both races working together in harmony. They all had one thought of helpfulness in mind, just as Mr. Lems had called his daddy, Uncle Vest, the

28

whites now called him Uncle Sunny. Because of the splendid record his family had in that community, he never asked a merchant for a favor and didn't get it.

Once Sugar Babe went up town and saw something on sale where her father used to trade. When she asked about it, the proprietor said, "If you are Vest Greene's daughter, you can get anything in my store. I never knew a finer man."

Yes, this was Dixie, the kind of place we all love and adore, for in it we find not the hypocrisy practiced in so-called liberal places. Here is real feeling among its people. Real friendship, and as Maw Lou often expressed it, "Honey, us got feeling for each other here and a real friendship that nothing can destroy."

"Of course, here we have plenty of room for improvement," Maw told Paw one day after visiting some of the old plantation hands. She had seen Uncle Friday, who was a deacon of the church. That Sunday he had prayed in church and in his childlike faith, he asked God to come to his relief. "Don't take time to saddle your horse, ride him bareback. Don't send your son 'cause you know how chillin is: they love to stop along the road and throw rocks. Please come yourself." Yes, this old deacon's faith was as real as the air he breathed, as plain as the nose on his face. He always said he talked with God like a natural man. Uncle Friday was one of the oldest men around in that community. He had become feeble in body but not in spirit. He was one of the few who went around in the neighborhood at night and told ghost stories. When Maw Lou's children were small, they were afraid for days after a visit from Uncle Friday.

Maw Lou was getting old and lonely. She missed Paw Vest more than ever, and the children had all gone their ways. She continued to keep Paw's old buggy and wagon under the shed of the old barn. She began to act strangely. One day she went out under the shed and sat in Paw Vest's buggy. There she sat for hours in the dusty, broken-spoked and spider-webbed buggy just looking out in space. Eve knew Maw was thinking of the time she and Paw shared so much as they rode together to church. When she came into the house, her cheeks were stained with tears. Eve told Mandy, Maw's niece, who was visiting: "She must be thinking of the days when she and Paw rode along the "big road' to church, laughing and talking all the way, while two of us children sat in the foot of the buggy with our little feet hanging out each side. Sometimes Maw held a baby in her lap while Paw tried to teach it to drive, letting it hold the lines. It isn't easy to give up someone you have shared life with for a quarter of a century."

Spring had come again. The flowers had begun to bloom around the borders of the yards of the humble farm folks. The dogwood, hay blossoms and honeysuckles made rough, early rising hunters pause in the woods for a look at nature as they sought their favorite game. The dear old South was all dressed up in nature's loveliest garment of flowers. The fields were equally beautiful with green coverlets of wheat, rye and oats. Here and there one could hear "geehaws," for men and boys were preparing the land for planting. Down by the woods in secluded places, women and children were weeding the white-covered tobacco beds. One could hear such songs as "I'm going to lay down my burdens, down

30

by the river side," and "I got my ticket signed for Glory."

One looking on and listening to these farm people singing, just continually singing, always singing, one wonders what is in their minds as they sing and toil. Are they singing to make their burdens lighter? Are they singing to keep back something a suppressed people cannot speak? Are they singing for the pleasure they get out of it? Are they singing because there is nothing else to do? Could one learn their reasons by learning more about the economic conditions under which most of them live?

The Negro in this country has enjoyed religion for generations. For a long time he felt that this old earth held no good things for him; that the good things of life belonged to someone else. He expected his reward in Heaven. Now, with the dawn of a new day in which he has been trained and become more intelligent, the Negro no longer wants his enjoyment in Heaven, but desires his share of earth's blessings. "For the earth hath He given to the children of men."

Eve was teaching her history class. She was reviewing the Negro progress since World War I until the present. "Oh, he has made tremendous progress in the South. You see, I was a young girl during that time and some teachers worked for twenty-five dollars a month. Maids were getting two dollars or a dollar and a half a week. Why, children, a man would plow a whole week for five or ten dollars and most times he took that up in groceries." Ruthie spoke up, "Miss Eve, how did the people live?" "Well, they lived poorly when it came to having nice homes. Few owned homes. You did not see fine cars then like you and your parents own today. No nice

31

schools in the country. We had little huts for schools with one little stove in it; no lavatories. Oh, it was awful."

"Miss Eve, how did you get to school?"

"I walked about five miles to school every day. I helped gather wood to keep warm. I took my turn warming my hands over the little stove where more than fifty others warmed. Sometimes we covered the floor with a sack where the teacher sat to keep out the cold that was coming up through the hole in the floor." Eve's class sat spellbound as she related the progress the Southern Negro had made since 1900.

Eve dismissed her class and rushed home to see about Maw Lou. She had been sitting in the dusty old buggy most of the afternoon. She told Eve: "I dreamed about your Paw last night. I thought he came in while I was sitting on the bed in my gown. He asked me to take the end of my gown and wipe the teardrops that fell from his face as he lay dying. He said it was still there and he couldn't rest as long as it stayed."

Eve suggested that Maw leave the old surroundings, but she was reluctant to leave the old plantation of the Southland. She was a part of it and was determined to live in the South 'til the end of her days. She told the children when they insisted on sending her away: "I'm not goin' nowhere to live in my old days. Got much right here as that old branch down there in the woods and it was here long before I came here. It's here to stay and so am I. I'm going out to Mr. Lems' old place to stay awhile with Mandy, my niece. You know I helped raise her after my sister died. She is just like you, Eve, like my own youngun." They knew when Maw said a thing she meant it.

32

CHAPTER IV

The Cry of War Is Heard

PEARL HARBOR had been attacked and there was the cry of war. Bill, Eve's husband, was one of the first to volunteer. He had served as a youth in World War I. Eve did not want Bill to leave her now and, too, she thought: "He doesn't have to go. He just feels it's his duty to go." So she at last gave in and told Bill to go where duty called.

Eve was more lonesome than she had ever been. She longed for Bill with all her heart. She knew he had finished his basic training and would soon be on his way to the Pacific theater of war. She knew he wanted to help fight the war that they were fighting to end all wars. Bill was happy when time came to go. As he lay on his bunk while his ship was tossed and rocked by the waves of the Pacific Ocean, he was thinking and praying, praying for the safety of himself and the men on board while convoy ships surrounded them and protective airplanes hummed overhead. Bill was thinking as never before and hoping that the "Government for the people and by the people" would not perish from the earth.

The Negroes were a part of the great country he loved, as distinctly so as her great mountains, rivers and lakes. They came with Columbus; they went with Perry to the North Pole. They tramped with

Washington during the Revolution. Crispus Attucks was the first to give his life for a free America. Bill thought that surely his people should be treated fairly within her borders.

In his heart was a song. For years his people before him had learned to sing their troubles to the Lord. It seemed to him that God made the Negro with a store of songs in his heart for all occasions, sufficient for any situation. Wherever he is, he can sing and out of his sincere singing comes many kinds of deliverance.

When Eve heard from Bill, he was somewhere safe in the Pacific. Oh, how glad she was! It seemed as though she had been shut up in a box and the lid now was lifted. She lived through endless days and eternal nights before the letter came. His safety, his love meant more to her than anything on earth. He seemed near as she read his letter, yet so far away. Standing there feeling the presence of his love so real, she thought she heard him whisper as he had done when he came home during World War I while he was courting her: "You are so young, warm and sweet. Yes, beautiful!" He had said those words the first time they met and they still lingered in her heart as she stood there in the bleak and lonely world without Bill. Tonight she would live life all over again with him in the land of her dreams. They would stroll together in the meadow, visit the old millpond, picinc together under the dark pines near Shady Grove. He would look into her big, brown eyes, and she would blush the way she did years ago. He would laugh a devilish, happy little laugh that always said, "I caught you off guard." They would hold hands and stroll while he told her how much he cared. She would hear Maw Lou calling: "Eve,

34

it's time to go. Come on." Embarrassed, she would
tell Bill goodbye while they planned another tryst.
She remembered how she felt about him when she
married, and how through the years their love was
like an ivy vine clinging closer and closer; and how
she waved farewell to Bill as he boarded the train,
hoping and praying that God would bring him back
to her.

Eve waved farewell to Bill as he boarded the train, hoping and
praying that God would bring him back to her.

She knew Bill was a "soldier." He loved his country. He had written and told her of the many things
he had witnessed and experienced "over there" and
concluded by saying, "Our country with the freedom
of the individual; yes, freedom of speech, freedom

of worship with all its opportunities is surely worth fighting for."

Eve left home the next day to visit Maw Lou at Mandy's house in the country.

There she found Mandy's two children picking cotton, and she went into the field with them for a while in the afternoon. She talked with Vicky and Little Bud who had been kept out of school to pick cotton. Little Bud was not at all pleased. She overheard him tell Vicky: "When I get a man, I am going to be a doctor like Doctor Jay if it is the last thing I do. I am tired staying out of school picking cotton."

"Vicky, who was very fond of Jim, her daddy, began to defend him: "Little Bud, you know us ain't got nothing. That's why Paw got to keep us outer school to pick cotton. Maw says Paw is a fool to work all these years and then don't have nothin." Little Bud thought for a while and then said, "Reckon you right. Paw must can't help hisself with all us to take care of and then he didn't get a chance to go to school. Seems like that would be reason enough for him to send us. He knows how hard it is to live when you can't make much. I want an education. That's all."

Little Bud didn't know that his own State had planned not only to see that all children attend school, but that all the schools in the State were to be worthy of the name. Surely he would get an opportunity to attend high school right where the little one-room school sat by the side of the road. A social change was taking place in the old South. After the Korean conflict it seemed that the Negroes had surely emerged from a state of insecurity to a sure faith in themselves.

Little Bud and Vicky along with others were learn-

ing all kinds of skills at camps. They were develop-
ing poise, faith in themselves and in others, resource-
fulness, creativity.

Eve and Maw had come back to Warrenville
where Maw Lou seemed like a "fish out of water."
She had lived out in the country with Mandy and all

"Little Bud, you know us ain't got nothing. That why Paw got
to keep us outer school to pick cotton. Maw says Paw is a fool to
work all these years and then don't have nothin'."

the sweet memories of the past lingered in her heart.
She visited old Deacon Friday who was ill. She and
others had prayed with him. Seeing how sick he was,
Maw Lou stayed there with her old friend Aunt Zil-

37

phia until he died and helped get everything washed and cleaned up.

It was a custom in that community for everybody to go to what they called the "setting up." Aunt Molly, another oldster on the plantation, whispered to Aunt Zilphia, "How did Brother Friday die? Did he die hard?" "No, he asked me to move the pillow from under his head. When I did that he smiled and slipped away," Aunt Zilphia replied with tears in her eyes. "I know Brother Friday was going to Heaven. He is just waiting for Reverend Eli to dismiss his spirit from the body. Then he is going to fly all over God's Heaven."

Sis Dora, who was sitting over in the far corner of the room, beckoned for Aunt Molly who hastily joined her. Whenever one died in this community, all the past and present of the dead were discussed. Aunt Molly was one of the older generation and was a specialist in that field. She said, "I done tell you long time ago Friday had come back to the fold. You 'member that time they had him up in church meeting 'bout Brother Timmons's wife? Well, after then he started going straight." Sis Dora spoke then, "I believe he got shame in that church meeting. You know they called it specially for him. Then he got kinda poorly and couldn't get out much like he use to, only occasionally to the church. I believe he made it all right."

Just as they finished talking, they heard a large clap of thunder. Everybody in the room looked at each other. Sis Molly was first to speak: "Hope it don't rain tomorrow 'cause everybody will think Brother Friday is lost." She had hardly finished when Sis Dora reminded her that when Deacon Friday was baptised, a snake was in the creek. She was

38

whispering, "You know there was a great big water moccasin in Belly Ache Branch the day old Reverend Mixon was preaching here about thirty-five years ago. It started toward the place where Parson Mixon was baptising him. Brother Friday was hollering, 'Wait there, Rev!' but before he knowed it, Parson Mixon had dipped him and washed all his sins away right there in Belly Ache Branch. The snake just struck right out for shore and got out the way before the next one was carried into the water. After then lots of folks didn't have no faith in him, but I always could see some good even though things didn't always look just right. He had plenty of time and all been praying. Us can tell by tomorrow if it be raining. You know they say a soul is lost in Hell if it rains during the funeral. 'Spect they going to have a powerful big crowd at church 'cause everybody here knowed Brother Friday and he is well liked."

Again Aunt Molly reminded her of how trifling Deacon Friday worked his farm. "He worked all his life and never seemed to be any better off for it. He just as well moved up the road with his children. He mighta live longer I 'spect. I am sorry for poor old Aunt Zilphia. Don't know what go 'come of her. She is a good old soul and so 'voted to Brother Friday."

By this time Aunt Sally, Aunt Zilphia's sister, had joined the whispering group. It was she who said: "Spect Zilphia will be spiking at Old Deacon Timmons; he's a widower, you know. He just lost his wife last summer and he is right spry yet."

She was interrupted by Aunt Molly. "Why, Sally, did you ever see a man as old as Brother Timmons marry a woman his age? I bet he's got his eyes on some of these young girls 'round this place. That's why he tries to step like a boy, but when you look at

39

him in the back and see the bend in his knee, you can tell he got right good age on him."

The next day the funeral was held at Shady Grove Baptist Church. All the people from miles around

Uncle Friday asked God to come to his relief. "Don't take time to saddle your horse, ride him bareback, and don't send your son, 'cause you know how chillin is. They love to stop along the road and throw rocks."

came to pay their respect. The Rev. Eli preached a wonderful sermon, after which the choir sang "Shall We Gather at the River," while they were viewing the body. Sis Dora looked out the window and, behold! by the old pump, grazing on the grass that grew around, was "Old Gray," Deacon Friday's old mule. He had followed behind the procession

40

from the house where he had been left grazing on the new hay in the cotton patch. "Lord Mercy, did you ever see anything like that? Yes, everything loved Brother Friday. Even the old mule came to the funeral. Bet he is at rest today, turned out to be so clear and bright.   *   *   *

Eve had begun teaching again and Maw Lou was alone at the house, except when she visited the farm, and that was every time she had the chance. The old buggy under the shed had worn with the years just sitting there. One day after Eve had gone to work, the old lady went out under the shed in the cool of the evening and sat in the old cobwebbed, dusty, broken-spoked-wheel buggy in which she and Paw Vest had ridden many a loving, happy mile in and around that community. As she sat there so wrapped up in the past, surely one looking on could see how lonely life is with no one to love. Heaven must have hid its face at the sight of the sad, old lady, and angels must have wept.

The next morning, while sitting at the breakfast table, Maw's enlarged picture fell from the wall and the glass in the frame broke into many, many pieces. Ruthie and Eve looked at each other. Maw Lou was the first to speak. "Uh-uh. I told you something gwine happen to me." Eve tried to assure her by telling her that any picture worn or improperly hung was liable to fall.

That night Maw Lou dreamed she was out in the ocean alone in a boat. She was so afraid and then she saw a man in white with an outstretched hand guide her to the shore. There she found Paw Vest sitting and waiting for her. They embraced and suddenly each had on two wings; and soon they flew away to Heaven where they could be at rest.

41

She got up and told Eve, "I am going to the old Lems' plantation for the last time. I can't leave 'doubt going back there. We were so happy there."

She visited her friends in the little old house where she was born. It had been remodeled but still brought back fond memories. It seemed as if she could hear the voices of those passed on calling to her to join them.

When she returned home, she told Eve to send for the other children as she felt sick. Eve called in the doctor, who told Eve: "She is worn out and, too, she hasn't the will to live. She told me she was homesick." "The world is changing too fast," she said, "too fast and getting weaker, too. We used to have real love around here, but seems like we are losing something dearer than all our possessions. I want to go home to my Lord." Dr. Jay had hardly finished telling Eve when Sunny called them to the room. He and Eve got there just in time to see Maw Lou smile and bid farewell to the troubles of this old world. Yes, she went to join the great reunion in the Promised Land. It was a heartbroken group that returned to Eve's house after Maw's passing, yet they realized life must go on.

The school was celebrating Negro History Week. Mr. Brice from Ohio had been invited to speak. A former student at Warrenville, he told them about the many Negroes in the rural and urban districts who know little about the good things of life. "They work and get little for their labor, yet they seem satisfied. They are looking for a brighter day. The day for which you are looking here, but you have to be trained to accept, appreciate and make good with the present opportunities." He told them about outstanding Negroes.

Just then Aunt Zilphia looked up and recognized him as Sis Dora's eldest son whom she hadn't seen since he went to Ohio to live with an aunt after his father's death. She looked up, pushed her kerchief farther down under her hat, straightened her glasses

As she sat there, so wrapped up in the past, surely a person looking on could see how lonely life is with no one to love. Heaven must have hid its face, at the sight of the sad, old lady, and angels must have wept.

and whispered to Aunt Molly, "Ain't dat Dora's boy, old Zeke? Well, if I hada knowed that, I never woulda come here tonight."

43

Mr. Brice continued, "Every well-thinking Negro knows that we cannot solve our problems in a day. It will take close, sincere cooperation of our white friends if our problems are to be solved. No two races can live side by side and truthfully say that neither has any need of the other. In some way and to a great degree each is dependent on the other." Brother Timmons, who always answered the preacher on each Sunday at this point struck the floor with his cane, "Go on, Man; you preaching now."

After the interruption the speaker said, "The Negro problem is not a Southern problem. It is a national problem. Riding through the South it seemed to me you are more progressive here than any section I have visited. May I conclude by saying it's a privilege to come back to Warrenville and see the wonderful progress you are making here. Your wonderful schools, playgrounds, swimming pool are a credit to any community."

Eve was so proud of Mr. Brice, because "He is one of the home boys," she told the audience.

44

CHAPTER V

Return to the Plantation

THE Korean War was over and the boys had returned. Many had given their lives that others might live. The community was proud of the record some of the boys had made.

Aunt Molly said one day to Sis Dora: "Did I eber think I'd see the day when a Negro would be an officer in the Army! I kin hardly believe my eyes. I 'member well when the boys left in World War I. Now, this is the third one I've seen and what a wonderful change has taken place. I tell you we are certainly improving. Look at the nice houses and schools. Even we got whole communities owned by Negroes. The little red houses have disappeared almost completely. God sure been good to us."

Sis Dora didn't answer. She was sitting with joyful tears in her eyes and a thanksgiving prayer in her heart. Her grandson, Little Bud, who used to quarrel about being kept out of school to pick cotton and had vowed he would be a doctor like Dr. Jay, was one of the returning vets. Now he would complete his education. He would become one of the best doctors Warrenville had ever had. Instead of the little house he was reared in, his father Jim had bought them a nice home, and now he was really proud of his dad, who had taken advantage of the

the new social change with its improvements among the Negroes of the Southland.

* * * *

Eve and Bill planned a vacation in the West. They, too, were getting along in years. They had seen many changes made. Eve liked to tell about her childhood days when she and Bill sat alone on the long winter nights by the open fireplace that she cherished so because it reminded her of the happy times on the old plantation.

"Do you remember Uncle Richard, like Uncle Friday, went around among the neighbors at night, telling about the ghost he had seen? Well, one night he came to our house and said he met a dog. Soon the dog turned to a man. After he got to the old creek where you crossed the creaking old, wooden bridge, it turned to a big horse and started chasing him. Well, Bill, I never was so afraid in my life. Paw sent me to get him a glass of water and the pail set out on the wooden shelf by the pump on the porch. When I got there, seems like the top of my head flew off, I was so afraid."

Bill interrupted, "What did you do?"

"Why, I screamed and all came running out to see what was the trouble. I thought I saw a hand reaching out for me. To this day I don't really know what happened, I was so afraid."

Bill laughed and said, "Even now as old as I am, a ghost story like that kinda makes me feel creepy all over."

Eve continued to explain how she got even with Uncle Richard. "He always sat in the same rocking chair at our house so I got me some long pins and went under the chair and stuck them through the thin cushion. When he sat on them, it made him very

46

angry and he tried hard to find out who did it. Nobody knew. Maw and Paw swore they would find out for him and punish the guilty, but it was impossible because no one knew but me. Hence, they lost their good friend's weekly visits to my great relief."

"I see, you were pretty mischievous," Bill added with a sly grin.

"Well, I like to think about the old times too, and especially the night Paw Vest thought the Germans were coming. It was the first time he had heard dynamite and he thought it was a bomb. You know that was my first week at home on a furlough. I was outdone with Sunny when it happened. He came running out of the house with the baby in his arms and Maw Lou and the small children followed. 'Come on, you all,' he said, 'the Germans are coming!' If I hadn't been there, I bet you all would have spent the night in the swamp."

Bill looked at Eve. She was smiling but there was a serious look in her eyes. She was thinking of Paw and of how they had worked to protect their children from the hardships of life. How Paw had taught that the time would come when they would be compelled to stand on their own feet. How he had said, "The world doesn't owe you anything. You must work for what you get." How he had looked at her the day he put her on the train to go to college and said, "Whatever you do, be honest, be decent. If you don't have but one change of clothes, put them off at night and wash them. Put them on the next day with your head up and keep plugging."

There were tears in her eyes as she sat there thinking and wishing how wonderful it would have been if Paw Vest could have lived to see the results

47

of his training in the lives of his children. How happy he would have been!

Yes, the community in which he had lived and preached loyalty, honesty, thrift and love of one's fellowman had been made better because Paw Vest lived in it. Yes, it was not an uncommon thing to hear some of the older ones use the expression, "Yes, like Vest Greene used to say, we better learn to work together and try to own something of value and not be dependent all our days on others."

With widespread social, economic, political and moral changes each coming in conflict with the other, sure the whole world needs to practice the doctrine of working together in order that these conflicts will be kept at a minimum, if chaos is to be averted, Eve thought as she and Bill sat talking over the past.

She remembered the time Paw Vest took her and Mernera to meet their cousin Sue who had come to Warrenville on an early morning train. When Sue saw them she came running across the railroad tracks and tumbled, spilling the half-gallon tin bucket of molasses Maw's sister had sent her. It took considerable time cleaning Sue up since her face, hair and clothes were matted with molasses. Eve had to laugh every time she and Bill talked about it.

"Really, I think that is one of the funniest things I ever saw. My, how the man in the little station laughed. That was as funny as when I was coming home my first Christmas from college. I had my school banner across my shoulder and one on my suitcase. Oh! I was so proud, stepping with my head up and not seeing where I was going. I felt like a was walking on air. Then suddenly I stepped on a banana peeling and over I went with the contents of my suitcase scattered everywhere and the train

48

ready to pull out; but some kind people helped me up and gathered my things for me. From that day until now I always watch where I am going."

Bill laughed and said, "I bet that wasn't as funny as it was embarrassing."

Eve retorted: "You bet! Why I could hardly hold up my head. You see I fell backward. Bill, you can't say a thing. I never will forget the day in the spring after we were married that you went fishing and began to nod under the old willow tree that stood over that deep fishing hole. Sunny said when you fell in, you did not know what had really happened until he and Bun were pulling you ashore."

"Yes, Honey," Bill said. "That's a day I will never forget. I think we have talked enough for one night and mostly about the past. Let's go to bed."

Next morning Bill was up bright and early. He planned on going hunting. "Look here, Honey," he called to Eve, "You had better do like your Maw used to do for your Paw." "What's that?" Eve asked. "Throw an old shoe at me for luck." Eve laughed and said, "Do you know it always worked with her. I guess it was because she believed. Any way, I will try it. It's real fun to recall some of the things Maw and Granny believed, like throwing salt in the fire to stop an owl from hollering, or someone was coming when a spider came down in the house; bad news when a rooster looked away from the house and crowed; death whenever a dove came into the yard; fresh meat when the soot on the back of the chimney burned; and to top it all, Maw nailed little new pieces on the house when Paw died to keep him from coming back to frighten us."

"Uh-huh," Bill began to laugh and say, "Yes, but he waited on her down by the woods and nearly

49

frightened her to death, she said. I think I have heard enough. Bye, Honey. Wish me luck." And off to the woods he went for the rest of the day.

P.T.A. was to be at eight o'clock that night so Eve had to practice a group of children for a playlet that night. She had them singing, "Oh, dear, what is the matter with you, dear." The others who seemed unhappy would answer, "The parents won't visit the school." She was trying to interest the parents in keeping in touch with their children's progress. She also wanted them to discuss their problems with her. Eve believed firmly that there were few bad children but many bad parents, and that the only way to improve and help the children was to improve and help the parents. She felt that the proper training and stability of the home was one weak chain in the development of her people. She always told the parents at the P.T.A. meetings that the home was the most important place in our civilization; therefore, it is the most sacred. From it every other organization springs. To think how many people neglect their home! They fail to guide and direct in the right path the little children that God gives them. They put any and everything before the home. Eve knew that if the Negro ever comes into his own, he must be trained and that training must come from the homes.

She remembered an expression Maw Lou taught them. "Manners will carry you where money won't." She had experienced that. She had seen people with money whose behavior was so bad no one wanted to be bothered with them. Eve knew that the leaders of her people had a great task before them if they prepared their people to share equally in the social, political and economic changes. She knew it would take lots and lots of time to prepare them. She often said. " If an army is unprepared and gains ground, doesn't have the proper weapons to hold out when the enemy overtakes them, it loses what it has gained and falls victim to the stronger forces. Let us not go on emotions. Let us gather the necessary weapons of life and then we won't have to retreat or fall victims to circumstances."

CHAPTER VI

'Home Is Where the Heart Is'

THE years had brought many changes in that little community. All the elders had passed on to a fairer land, except Aunt Molly. It was Eve's and Bill's custom to visit the old plantation several times during the year. When they arrived at Aunt Molly's house, she was seated in a chair under an old oak tree near the little, faithful black wash pot which, if it could have talked, would have told a story of all the families for three generations, clothes it had so carefully and patiently boiled to a beautiful snow whiteness that only a pot of its kind could have done. It would have told of happy children raking and gathering chips from the woodpile to keep up her steam for parties and night suppers for the plantation friends when they filled her with fish stew and rice. Many of them had gone away and left the little pot sitting there on bricks. It could not count the number of bricks it had worn out while serving each generation. It just sat there as a memorial to a wonderful past.

Aunt Molly pushed up her kerchief from over her eyes, took her spects and wiped them in her large gingham apron, placed them securely over her eyes and looked up the road at the car that was coming. "Sho' believe that's Bill and Eve. Ain't seen them fur over a month." She turned to her little great-granddaughter and ordered her to sweep off the porch, " 'Cause her teacher's coming.''

"Yes, you still love your peanuts," Eve said after greeting the old lady, who was using the paddling block near the wash pot to beat up her pinders. She told Eve, "I can't chew them like I used to so I keep my tobacco sacks that I buy smoking tobacco in to put dem in after I mash dem with dis here hammer."

After spending a while chatting with Aunt Molly, they walked down in the woods where the old millpond was. Bill laughed as he thought of the times when he and others carried corn in a sack to have it ground, and brought back a peck of grits and sometimes meal. The weeds and bushes had grown around the old building. Most of its sides and flooring were gone, but the old pond or creek was still there. As Bill and Eve stood there alone, looking back through the years, Bill put his arms around Eve and began to sing:

> "I wandered today to the hill, Maggie,
> To watch the scenes below.
> The old rusty mill is still, Maggie,
> As it was in the days long ago."

He stopped and they walked back to Aunt Molly's and had dinner, and after walking up to the Lems' old mansion, they went back to Warrenville. Eve was the first to speak: "Bill, we have been East, North and West, but nothing gives me the happiness that can compare with a visit to the old plantation. I believe everybody who ever lived on one as we did loved it."

Bill didn't speak. He was thinking of the two wars in which he had served, of the people and places he had seen, and how anxious he had been to get back home and settle in this community after finishing his education. Now, he was ready to retire. Eve's sister, Helen, who lived in California, wanted them to come West. Bill told Eve he had no intention of pulling up stakes and going west. Eve agreed that they were perfectly happy in Warrenville.

"We have Ruthie and her children. What more can we ask?" Eve finally said. "You know I am expecting her two boys for the weekend." Bill looked up from his paper. "You mean "Butch' and 'Mity Mite' are coming? Well, the two boys are a complete recipe for a racket," he finished with a smile, to which Eve replied: "Bill, there is nothing wrong with 'Butch' and 'Mity Mite' that you didn't outgrow. "You outgrew quite a few things yourself. Do remember the day your mother bought you a new dress and you slipped to church early to show it and when you got there, no one was there to see it. You had forgotten that preaching was held only twice a month. You didn't tell me that one," Bill concluded.

Eve was laughing a sheepish little laugh because she did not know that Maw Lou had told Bill about it. She soon changed the subject by calling Bill's attention to his "lodge meeting." "Well, I see you are anxious to get rid of me. What's up?"

Eve dropped her book on the table, went over to the lounge where Bill lay and embraced him and said, "Honey, you know I never want to get rid of you. Do you remember the poems I sent you when we were so far apart?" With her head on his shoulder and arm still around his neck, she recited:

> "As long as I have you
> And you have me,
> There is nothing that can come
> Between us two."

54

Bill didn't speak for a while. He was thinking of just how much those very words had meant as he lay in the foxholes in the Pacific. When he spoke, he told Eve, "You are the reason I am alive. Your laughter, love, faith, ideals! Well, a fellow just couldn't give up with a wife like you. We are both along in years and today you are as pretty to me as you were when you were sixteen."

Tears were in Eve's eyes now and Bill turned her face up and kissed her as he stroked the locks of her silver hair.

Just as he opened the door to go to "lodge meeting," the moon was unusually beautiful. He called Eve there on the steps. They stood like two kids in love's embrace, looking at the bright, shining moon. Bill said, "The moon makes me think of striping sugar cane in the moonlite. Then jumping ditches and hayrides." He called the moon a "warm, bright Southern moon." Eve called it a "love moon."

"You know, standing here I think of the old apple orchard, the time when we would roll down the hillside to the old camp-meeting ground that we held sacred." She went on talking as Bill stared into the great beyond. "Yes, Honey, we must cherish and hold dear the sacred things of life. For there are enemies within and without who wish to destroy our way of life. They would destroy the individual freedom by stirring up strife among nations and people."

At last Bill spoke: "Yes, when we see the cover moving about in human affairs, it's always wise before jumping to conclusions to turn the cover back and see what's under it. We are living in a wonderful age. Let us join with others in helping to make it a place where God is supreme in the lives of the people. Let us get joy out of serving others. Let us believe in the present with all its opportunities, in the future with its promises."

With those words, Bill turned around on one foot and said, "I am not going out tonight. We have something to do here. Plan a meeting with the parents at school. They are the ones to train if we are to help rear the children who need us most."

That night on retiring they prayed for a world community where all men would be brethren, yes, and have an opportunity to make glad dreams come true.

CHAPTER VII

'Few and Far Between'

THE next morning Bill was up bright and early. When Eve asked, "Why are you up so early?" he replied, "The early bird catches the worms."

After breakfast, Bill drove the car around and loaded it with cosmetics. He had work to do. First, he would stop at Aunt Molly's and have a chat. She always had something worthwhile to say, so this morning was no exception. She had just gotten her second cup of black coffee and gotten out in the shade of the old oak tree. Bill could see the smoke from her pipe as he turned the curb around the patch of woods near her yard. When he drove in the yard, the old lady got up to meet him.

"Lawd Mercy! Here's Fesser. Sho' glad to see you. Did you bring my gal?"

Bill told her Eve was out late at P.T.A. last night and did not feel up to taking the trip.

"Sho' look for her. I ain't seen her in a long time. You know da is a lot happening here since you was here last. Why, you 'member the old man dat lived down in a cave by der river. Well, he dead now."

"You mean the old man they called 'Yankee Bill'?"

"Yes, dat was the only name he ever had. You see hit was like dis. His mammy was fourteen years

57

old at the close of the war between the States. I mean dat one whar de Yankees was concern. Well, when dey came through, the Missus and Mister left the house in her charge late one evening. She tell me years ago 'ofer she died dat a soldier rode up to du big house, a Yankee soldier wid lots of pretty bottons in his blue shirt. He ordered his men to get down and they tuck over the place fur the night, ordered her to fix vittles and then to make him a bed up in der top story of the house. She was up dar making the bed, scared to death, when dis big man who was de boss came in and threw her across der bed and when der baby was born, she named him 'Yankee Bill.' She didn't know der man's name. He didn't tell her. She didn't know who he was. He left after breakfast the next morning, taking his men wid him."

Bill sat stunned. He had always wondered why the old man lived as a hermit down by the river. The school children used to laugh at him when he came to town to gather food and junk. He never bothered anybody, wore his hair long and was always alone. Bill thought it must have been an awful life alone and that death must have brought "Yankee Bill" a welcome relief. Aunt Molly continued talking.

"Yes, dey found him dead in his cave. Dey say he had his mammy's picture on de wall and found some drawings he had done looked lake a Yankee soldier. You know, he couldn't read or write. His old mammy tell years ago der fust day he went tu school the children laughed when du teacher asked him his name and he said 'Yankee Bill.' She could not get him to go back to dat little school dat use to set 'way back side dem wood over dere." Aunt Molly pointed out the directions while Bill looked on.

"Fesser, you know his mammy never married. She said she was afraid of every man dat come around her. She was a queer old lady who never got over the way she had 'Yankee Bill.' No wonder he grew up and went tu the bank of dat river and built his cave house. You could see him fishing out there all during the year. Den he would peddle them around here to get money tu buy vittles. Sometimes he picked berries and sell dem. I 'member when he was young, the gals tried to catch his tension but he was as scared of gals as his mammy was of men. Guess he in Glory now cause he never done a body no harm. He would cut wood fur you or help you bring in du cows or any other thing you ask him to do, if he weren't fishing"

Bill listened with sympathy for a man who had lived in a world of his own, a lonely world, a friendless world, a loveless world. He always heard true and strange stories when he visited Aunt Molly who was nearly at the century mark and could boast of being able to thread her needle without her glasses. She had a wonderful memory. Although a little slow expressing things, she never was "mixed-up" as she said her mind was clear. This morning she was in a story-telling mood. She told Bill about the time a stepmother in the community whipped her stepdaughter in the cotton field near the graveyard where the child's mother was buried. When they got back to their home, the stepmother's picture jumped down off the wall and danced on the floor, then crashed. After that for four days everything in the house jumped and danced around. Some broke; others remained unbroken. She finished by saying:

"I saw dat myself. I wus one uf de first people to git dare. Folks come from miles around to see dem cans, fruit jars, chairs and every other thing dance and jump around in that house. I tell you I don believe dat child ever got another whipping. I can't say 'cause dey moved away after den. Hit most as bad and frightening as Dilly's old boy Pete. Why he had a spell of fever. After he got well, a voice cum in him. When he would play too much, hit would tell him tu be quiet. People would pile in the house so you couldn't see Pete to hear dis thing talk. One day dey called in old Dr. Free and der thing begin to tell Dr. Free something about hisself. So hit scared him and Aunt Dilly couldn't git a doctor to come dere. Dat thing was sumpthing. Hit told people all dey ever done. Why, hit scare poor Pete to death. When he died, his mammy said, 'Dat's the first rest he had in months. The thing's talked all day if he was awake and late at night till the people left. Oh! Fesser, I done seen sumpthing in dis place since I been here," to which Bill admitted with a smile and and nod of his head.

Just then a car came around the bend. "Oh!, Lawdy, dat my white folks. Dey cum to see me other week and bring fruits, vittles, just 'ply my needs, dat's all. You know I worked fur dem a long time, nursed and cooked. Now, I old and dey neber threw me away. Why dat baby girl uf theirs finished college dis year and she gaged to one uf dem big men in de Army. She was here last week; say she tell him she ain't gwine marry him unless he promise to take care of her and her old nurse. All see here what she brought me?" The old lady pointed to a basket of groceries as her white folks parked and got out of their car.

Bill knew that kind of friendship between people is not easily destroyed. He also knew that as long as

60

the Negro leaders and the Negroes with means fail
to create jobs for their people, there can be no soli-
darity among Negroes in America. The majority of
them will not "bite the hand that gave them bread."
He knew that greedy politicians would use the
Negro as a means to an end. Bill had told Eve once
when they were discussing the Negro problems,
"You know the average Negro leader who has gotten
up in the world has tried to imitate white and leave
his race. He doesn't even know what the little man
is like and the pitiful thing about Negroes, most of
them belong to the little-man class. Let us say
seventy-five percent. When I came here to teach, you
know they tried to use me to foster segregation here
by wanting me to give honors to the light children
whether they deserved it or not. Too, there were certain people whose children were to get special consideration while the children who really needed to
feel a sense of belonging and have an opportunity
to learn things that their home life could not afford
be neglected. I had a hard time letting them know
that as long as I was principal, there would be no
distinction here in Warrenville High School. Perhaps if the school here had been controlled exclu-
sively by Negroes, I would have been gone a long
time ago."

"What became of the teacher who wanted all the
Majorettes light with long hair?" Eve asked.

"Well, she was fair and didn't like black children.
She wouldn't give them a chance. I observed her
selection one year and had a conference with her.
It made her angry and she resigned at the end of the
the term, but as the kids say 'I wasn't about to have
that sort of thing' here in Warrenville, and it was
good that she did resign. You see our Majorettes

61

are picked on ability. We have as good or the best in the county, as good as any in the State. We are proud of them. They are proud of themselves."

"Darling," Bill went on to say, "I don't mean to say that we don't have sincere, dedicated leaders. Sure we do, but they are 'few and far between.' As your mother used to say, many start out sincere and end up in the general 'racket of things.'

CHAPTER VIII

The Ways of the Home Folk

NEXT day they drove out to visit Brother Simon, one of Warrenville's oldest and most respected citizens. He was out at the barn, watering his mule. Eve stopped and sold his granddaughter some cosmetics while Bill visited with the old man. "Show did enjoy myself at der meeting der outher night. Hit was just lake I been saying. Us want good pay fur what us do and justice in de courts of de land and want us things to be as good as anybody else's, but us got plenty race pride and want to stay wid us race. Hit's der 'big nigger' dat wants to leave der race. He don count us little fellows no how."

Bill smiled and listened patiently as the old man went on. "If hit wus left to dem, we wouldn't git along as well as us do. You 'member when I lost my wife years ago? Well, she left me wid ten younguns, including a three-year-old baby. Hit was hard, rail hard wid me. One day I came out, didn't know where to turn. I looked east, north, west and south trying to figure my next step. Well, John Smith who owns the cafe down town, I went to him. He turned me down flat. I offered to mortgage my little home here to the colored bank. Made out papers, dey signed dem. Said dey would call me in a few days. Well, two weeks went by and I ain't hurd nuthing yit. I go down dere. The president tell me the board pass on papers and I could git du loan. He would call me next day and tell me when to come since papers was in his lawyer's office. Three more weeks passed. I ain't hurd nothing yet." Bill laughed and asked him if he ever got it.

"No, after den my son say, 'I am sorry, Paw. I vise you not to go dere. Let's try the First National Bank white.' Now, dat was on Friday. Tuesday der man call me and said, 'Uncle Simon, you can cum git your money. I did. Now, I do all my business dare. Dey treat me real nice."

Just then Eve called Bill to remind him of an appointment he had with a minister. On the way there they discussed some of the things they had heard and learned at Uncle Simon's house.

"You know people had segregated ideas a long time," Bill finally said. "Remember Miriam's attitude toward her brother Moses's wife?"

"Yes, I remember," Eve said. "I also remember reading of God's punishment of Miriam. There were also servants among them but God gave them rules by which they were to treat their servant."

"You mean to say there have always been servants and always will be, and that these people cannot look forward to being treated on an equality with their employer?" Eve laughed in an evasive kind of laugh, leaving Bill to fathom the answer.

When Bill spoke, it was after a long silence. "Yes, Eve, truly a social chain is in the making. The Negro is in the center of it. Something different, something real and lasting, for good will come out of it for both the Negroes and whites. Aunt Molly just said when we were there, that she was praying over it.

64

You know 'prayer opens a whole planet to man's activities'."

"Bill, I believe the great people on earth today are people who pray, not just talk about prayer, but put aside pressing matters and go aside and pray."

They were soon driving up to Rev. Eli's house. He was in his study and received them in his usual warm, friendly and joking way.

"Why, where did you get that old man you are with this morning?" he asked Eve, after greeting them both. Bill was accustomed to his jokes and admitted readily that he was the "old professor," as the folks called him around Warrenville.

"Yes, I am a bit concerned about my people and integration, but are they ready to be ushered into it without preparation. I, too, think it will be many, many years before some sections can be prepared. Yet I agree that the Negro needs more for his work, better opportunities along all lines so that he can develop properly. We have the answer to his problems, or may I say the correctability must come through education, through strengthened economic foundations and increased social responsibility. Human nature is plastic. Social customs are mutable. It is one clear lesson of history that new moral and new social habits follow changes in economic codes. I am afraid that our troubles too are largely due to the fact that each race too readily misunderstands and mistinerprets the other's conduct and aspirations."

Bill then asked "Rev. Eli, whom do you blame for race rioting and other illegal practices?" To which he said, "The responsibility does not rest upon hoodlums alone, but upon all citizens, white or black, who sanction force or violence in inter-racial rela-

65

tions or who do not condemn and combat the spirit of racial hatred thus expressed. You know in time everything will work out right if we have intelligent and sympathetic consideration by each race of the the other's needs and aims. Our purpose is to oppose propaganda of malicious and selfish origin and work for peaceful means of racial adjustment and understanding. We should boldly condemn anyone or organization who fosters racial antagonism in the South for you know from observation and experience regardless of what's been said or done, the Negroes have real friends among the white people of the Southland."

"Yes, Rev. Eli, my interviews every day with people have proven they feel that the white man here is a friend. Why, I met an old lady yesterday who gets a Government check and she won't trust anybody to cash it but the grocery store proprietor, and when she has letters to write, she goes to him to do her writing. In fact, Mr. Ludd looks after Aunt Mary and her affairs. She will tell you in minutes, 'Mister Ludd better tu me dan anybody I know. All dese nice things in my house him and Mrs. Ludd give 'em to me. Eber time she got her new ting she give me the outhers. Sometimes her bring me new tings too. I just love 'em. Been round dem all my life. Dey jest good people, dat's all.' "

"Yes, Bill, many Negroes, both young and old, feel the same way," Rev. Eli said after some thought. "I know one of our member's daughters who finished high school last year told my wife 'I had the prettiest dress of any in my class on class night. You know who bought it? The lady mother works for. She got it from that special fashion store for teenagers.' My wife said she looked lovely in the dress

66

and was beaming because her mother's boss bought it."

Just then the doorbell rang. Rev. Eli met a frightened little black boy who began talking as soon as Rev. Eli approached. "Reb, sis say please cum quick. Us live right round dere in Elbow Alley. You know Paw, he one of your deacons but he in jail and Maw fixing to have a baby. Sis say she want you to fetch dat uman who allus comes when Maw have her babies."

Rev. Eli scratched his head, trying to decide whether to go get Jim out of jail or go to see about Jim's wife. After a consultation with his own wife, he decided to get Aunt Malissa, official midwife of Warrenville, and talk with the officials about Jim. He was accustomed to getting Jim out of jail after a weekend spree when he had taken a little "nip," as Jim called it, and kept nipping beyond control.

Bill and Eve went home from Rev. Eli's house. Eve wanted to stop by an old lady's house who always told the kind of stories that left you laughing inside for days.

Soon as they were seated, Aunt Zella brought out a drink of homemade wine that she kept "specially fur hur friends," and began: "More things happening around here. Why right cross der road over dere da uman died last week. She want a bitta good. Why hur neber went tu church and she sell liquid to dem 'Surimes' and got one of dem in trouble about hur old gal one day call Stinking Pearl. Why der gal neber tuck a bath. Hur mammy say too much washing all over takes der strength away." Bill and Eve by this time could not look at each other for fear of laughing out loud, but Aunt Zella was unaware of that and continued. "Why, at hur funeral the preacher ain't know whut tu stay. Dey didn't have nary flower gal, nary pallbarrer, nuther did dey have anybody to read der dictionary over hur. She just wus a no good, dat's all."

Bill could hold it no longer. He had shuffled one foot and then the other to avoid laughing. He had to tell his own little joke for relief.

Aunt Zella hadn't finished. She never finished without telling a hair-raising ghost story. "Dis hear place is as hainty now as hit wus when I wus a child. Why, der other night coming from across the creek, I see a man behind me and Will. I tell Will to look back. Dat man didn't have on no head. Will call me foolish. Den I turned around tu look and der he wus done stretched out in der air high over der bridge. I say, 'Look, look! Will.' Just den he ducked low and disappeared. I tell you dis is a hainty place." She finished with a sigh to the great relief of all listening.

Bill and Eve loved these people with and for whom they had worked since receiving their education. They felt that the need was great in and around Warrenville for service to those who were less fortunate than they were. With that in mind they were always on the alert to be of service. They understood these people; their folkways and lores were a tradition handed down from generation to generation.

They often laughed about the funny eventful things they had seen and heard, like the mean old lady who wore a pocket in her skirt and one day the buttons jumped out of the skirt and flew around everyone's head in the room. They accused her of throwing them. Just then a spoon walked out of the kitchen, the water pail jumped off the shelf and danced around in the floor. This condition went on for days. People came to see and hear the story of an old lady possessed with the devil.

Then there was old Uncle Ervin who wouldn't go to church and took Sunday to raise the "roof off the house." One Sunday when he was at his best, using his most choice language, which wasn't fit for anyone to hear, something stuck its head out of the ceiling and gave a hearty Ha, ha, ha, ha. From that day on Uncle Ervin never cursed on Sunday.

They talked about the time Paw Vest stopped a a fight between two old deacons and their wives. Old Deacon Toney accused old Deacon Lundy of telling a lie about him. In the cotton field the next day old Deacon Tony kept singing "If you don stop your lying, God gwine cut out your lying tongue. God gwine cut out your lying tongue and hang it up and dry it." Old Deacon Lundy stood it as long as he could and then asked Deacon Tony if he was calling him a liar. The old deacon never replied but continued to sing. This proved too much for Deacon Lundy and he pulled off his cotton-picking sack and it wasn't long before both were rolling on the ground and cotton bolls were flying in every direction. As the fight continued, their wives got into it. "You say my husband tell a lie on your old man?" "You tell a lie yourself," Deacon Lundy's wife yelled to Deacon Tony's wife.

She being a smaller and older woman, tried to avoid a fight by saying, "Hit look lake a lie." This fired Mrs. Lundy to pitch heat and she hung her old "Baptist jacket" on a cotton stalk and the fight was on. Just then Paw Vest, who was also a deacon at the time, happened to be passing the cotton field and seeing the two women in an exposed position, being minus some needful undergarments during a warm early September, he tried to help by pulling their dresses over their exposed parts while he urged others to separate them. He always laughed and said, "Just time he had covered Sis Tony, Sis Lundy uncovered her." Paw Vest soon had the battle under control. In that spot of the big field there would be no more cotton to be picked that year. It was wrecked.

Rev. Eli had got Jim out of jail and he was talking like a child. When Rev. Eli told him his wife had a little boy, he said: "Just look at me. I jest sorry. Sally say I ain't no good, but I neber knowed what happened when I drink dat stuff Saturday. Some uf dem fellars are putting sumthing in dat drink so dey could steal all my pinders and fruit off de cart I had. I didn't know nuthing till I waked up in jail. I looked up at de loft and said: 'Oh, Lawdy, whare is I? Lawdy, whare is I at?'" Rev. Eli smiled as Jim continued to talk. "You know I use to be the biggest sport 'round here. Why, I could git de gals when 'dey wouldn't pay de outher fellars no tension."

"What did you do to make you a lady's man?" Rev. Eli asked, still amused.

"I see a lady at de church. I walk up tu hur and take off my hat and say: 'My name Jim Jones. May I see you safe tu your resident viding you ain't got no infections?'"

Rev. Eli could hold his laugh no longer for he thought that was a most unusual way to have been a lady's man. He soon had Jim home and, after admonishing him to live a better life, Rev. Eli left for home. He had been in Warrenville a long time and had preached out in the country at Shady Grove, but he had never met a more amusing person than Jim Jones. When he reached home and saw his wife and

70

new baby, he hollered: "Oh, Lawdy, here I been in jail and didn't even know I had a baby. Show oughta been hure. I reckon I jest ain't no good, but if you furgive me, Sally, dis will be my last drink." And from the look on Sally's face and the greeting she gave him, Rev. Eli thought as he rode home that if Jim had any sense at all he would stop drinking.

Elbow Alley got its name from its shape. The people who lived there were poor. The Alley was crammed with little three-room houses with no yard space and a very narrow street. In some of the homes as many as ten persons lived. They were a happy, working people, always ready to greet you with a friendly "How you feel?" or "How you all?" Rev. Eli visited his members there often and always left feeling better after being among these lowly people. They were a mixture of real life among the working Negro class. There was Aunt Classy who always made her granddaughter starch her wide petticoat real stiff and wash her several white kerchiefs. You could her her telling Stella "Starch my petty coats and iron dem good 'cause I gwine shout tomorrow and be show to wash my kerchiefs 'cause I gwine cry tomorrow. Hit Sunday, you know, and when Rev. Eli gits tu preaching, I gwine shout and cry fur my Lawd." Aunt Classy never missed a Sunday without singing, shouting and crying for her Lord.

There was Uncle Zeke who loved to see how many new songs he could learn and sing in church, so when he heard the boys singing "Alabama Bound," he liked it and Sunday couldn't come fast enough for him to sing it in church. It was the first Sunday and everyone was telling his and her experiences. So Uncle Zeke rose crying, face all drawn up in a frown, "I am Alabama Bound; I am Alabama

71

Bound. If you will go leave me here, I am Alabama Bound." Everyone, and especially the young people, began to laugh, to which Uncle Zeke, full of the spirit, responded, "You laugh at me as much as you please, but I am Alabama Bound." Brother Simon, who was more intelligent and could read well, got up and went over and sat behind Uncle Zeke. He pulled Zeke's coat tail and whispered to him: "Dat's a 'reel' you singing, Brother." While an amused audience looked on, the embarrassed Uncle Zeke took his seat. He said, "Dem boys hurd me a singing in der field and wouldn't tell me any betta. I'll fix de little rascals when I see dem tomorrow." That stopped Uncle Zeke's eagerness to sing new songs in church without knowing the meanings of them.

Then Old Sister and Brother Ben always sat in the amen corner and nodded. When Rev. Eli got in a high-preaching voice, they would wake up and Brother Ben would holler: "Gone, gone. Now, if you don stop, I gwine long wid you." His wife would sit nodding her head, hollering "To be show! To be show!

These were people who lived plain and simple, with a childlike faith in God and a love for all his creatures.

Rev. Eli always tried to help them by teaching them against superstition and ignorance. Once when he visited Aunt Classy she was all excited about her recovery from a recent illness. "Why, Reb., I was hurt by a oman dat use to lake my husband. I wus tu die in three day, but I went and seen Dr. Bozzard and he tell me to boil my 'you know what', and put sulphur and garlic in hit. I done dat and now I jest as good as new." Rev. Eli then knew what it was

72

that nearly took his breath away when he entered the room. He tried to explain to Aunt Classy that there was no truth in a thing of that sort, but she insisted that it was true and showed him a dime tied around her ankle that had turned black, a sure sign she had been poisoned, she believed.

Rev. Eli told his wife, Bill and Eve about this experience. They said that what the Negro leaders needed to do was to plan some types of program so that these people could be reached and helped. Rev. Eli said the church should take the first steps. Bill said the schools should play their part through parent organizations and classes. These people are too for behind to catch up immediately. It will take a long time to find a proper solution to their problem, and when and if that solution is found, it will take time and patience to make it work. "The first thing we have got to do is to see that their living standard is improved. Many of them are satisfied just as they are. They don't want to do or live any better," Bill told Rev. Eli. "Yes, I think that is what the Negro race needs as a whole to improve his economic status. He needs good jobs, good pay, good homes in which to rear his children. In fact, he needs economic freedom, not in the South alone because he's far better off here than any place I know, and having served in two wars abroad, I know a lot of places. We need economic freedom all over the United States and especially in the North and Northeast where certain meager jobs are never given to a Negro. They, of all places, have the most hypocritical way of segregating him when it comes to jobs or anything else for that matter, with but few exceptions."

73

All present at Bill's for supper that night gave their verbal approval of Bill's statement.

* * * *

Next week Bill and Eve left Warrenville to make their yearly visit to Eve's aunt in New York City who lived in Harlem. While there, they thought it queer to sit indoors with the doors barred, but Eve's aunt told them that it wasn't safe to leave doors unlocked at any time. In that section of Harlem it seemed that the Negroes, Spaniards and Mexicans were crammed together. Few whites lived there. You could hardly walk for the crowd and it seemed like the people didn't have much to do but stay in the streets. Bill and Eve were afraid to be out after dark. There were gangs, open protitution, dope fiends and every imaginable evil a person could see. Bill wondered how any organization in that city had time to clean up any other place without neglecting its duty to the people there. He told Eve one night, after a sightseeing trip all day through Harlem:

"Here you see everything: gang war, you see peace, segregation, desegregation and other social problems that threaten mankind. They can never be solved by any one group. It will take every organized group for good pooling their knowledge to even come near a workable solution of problems of the present situation and of all places where the need is great, I think it is right here in Harlem in New York City. When I compare the South, where we live, I feel like singing it's heaven on earth compared with this place."

Eve smiled and said "I am like Maw Jenny. Take me back to the old Southland. There let me live and die. Really, I am homesick. Let's leave tomorrow."

74

Eve meant that and no persuasion from her aunt could keep her longer.

When they arrived in Warrenville, Ruthie and the boys were there to meet them. There were the usual smiling faces of the bus boys, the friendly station manager and others that they had known for years and were glad to see them back in town. On the way home, Butch told Bill that "Mity Mite" had broken one of the Commandments to which "Mity Mite" asked "What I done?" "Why you told an untruth, that's what," Butch said. "Well, you broke one too. I don't tell one I broke. I bet you lie." "No." "How about stealing?" "No." "Well, I know one you done broke," "What was that?" "Bet you done committed adultry." At that "Mity Mite" was puzzled and looked from one of the grown-ups to the other for an answer while the amused parents ignored him completely. After all were home and the boys had been put to bed, Bill said to Ruthie: "My! 'Mity Mite' is being accused at the tender age of six of a serious charge," to which all laughed and prepared for bed. It was such a relief to be at home, away from the noise, racket and rush of the large-city life.

The next day Bill went to see a patron in Elbow Alley. The city inspector had been around and condemned the houses in Elbow Alley. Yes, the people there were going to have a new life. The little church was the only thing that wouldn't be torn down.

Yes, the South was continually improving the conditions of its colored citizens and as they discussed the progress Warrenville had made during the last twenty years, Bill said: "Nowhere has there been greater improvement among Negroes than here in the South. Beautiful homes, many with good jobs

75

and job opportunities still improving though there is lots to be done. If the people will get together, work together without selfish political ambitions, without a desire to rise at the little man's expense without using the ignorant lttle man to pull his chestnut out of the fire and then leave him with burnt fingers to do the best he can, as has been the case in so many instances. We will not need the Federal Government to enforce laws to integrate. The South can and will in time work out an amiable solution to its own problems. The South will not be forced, and if force is used, then it must be used to the limit and in the end we will find, as it was during the reconstruction, the white troops will be in sympathy with their Southern brothers."

"Yes, Bill," Eve said. "You are right. The Negro and white leaders here in the South should work together and make progress, so we need not get excited and forget that fact. Our friendship should be a real and lasting thing. As we work for better opportunities, it would be wise if we stop and pray this prayer when we see from whence we came or our forefathers came:

"Lord God of Hosts, be with us yet,
Lest we forget, lest we forget."

CHAPTER IX

Plantation Memories

O H! it seems that the whole world is in a storm of confusion. Instead of getting better, I sometimes feel it's getting worse. I am afraid we are all guilty of one thing," Eve concluded.

"What's that?" Bill asked, wholly amused at the seriousness of Eve.

"It's the Christlike spirit that inspired our forefathers. In reading the constitution you can readily see that they were men of spiritual wisdom who could see even down to our times and wrote laws that were good for all times," Eve finished with a deep sigh.

After a while, Bill spoke: "You know one of our greatest business men says he believes that a doctrine of separate racial business should mark the preliminary stages of the group's commercial progress, and that our ultimate goal should be to find an entree into the general economic fabric of the nation on a level of full and equal participation with other Americans."

"The challenge is ours to meet with courage and determination," Bill said. "Now for something. humorous."

Then smiling, he thought of an old joke Uncle Simon had just recently told him about the haunted house in which no one could live. Eve, looking at Bill's face, said, "Tell it. I know Uncle Simon told you a good one today while you all were out in the barn."

"Yes, he did at that," Bill replied. "Why he said that old log cabin across the creek used to be used by slaves. It was the only one left on the plantation. Every family which moved in it soon moved out. It seemed that the former tenants of long, long ago resent anyone who goes there to live. Mr. Ludd got that local preacher to move in. He is a widowed man, so he carried one of his deacons in there with him. The first night there he sat reading his Bible before retiring. Two big, black cats came in and sat down. After looking at each other for a while, one of the cats said to the other, "Where is Sadie? We can't start nothing till Sadie come,' Just then the old preacher put his Bible down and looked at the old deacon and said, 'I be damn if I am going be here when Sadie comes.' He started running while the old deacon tried to follow him. When he got near enough to talk to him, he asked, 'Reb, don't you think God wids us tonight?' To which Reb replied, 'If he is, he show is running.' "

"Oh, I love being around him. He keeps you laughing all the time with the quaintest and funniest stories. Where does he get so many from?"

Bill thought for a while and then said, "I reckon the old man was born in the closing years of the Civil War and has lived many of the stories he tells. He himself is a legend."

"Bill, I forgot to tell you about our club meeting last night. Well, someone invited our new neighbor who moved here from Pendelton. She is a real 'highbrow'. Why, she spent most of the evening telling us about how she entertained how many guests that she had at one sitting, and to top it all, she told us about the silver and pots, cake pans and dishes she owns."

Bill interrupted: "You mean to tell me a man's wife who teaches in a large institution doesn't know any better than that?"

"Wait, I haven't told you all. I was seated next to her and a minister's wife was seated across from her. She had the audacity to turn from me and tell the minister's wife, 'I want you to come see my things. In fact, I want to give some of my pans away. I know you appreciate things like that. I know you understand and can appreciate those kind of things.' Well, I never felt like telling anyone off in all my life as I did her. Why, she gloats and boasts more than a millionaire. Somewhere along the line she must have had it hard, poor thing, or else she is sick right in the head, I reasoned."

"Well, that's the trouble with most of our people who have an opportunity to get ahead. They figure nobody hasn't got anything or knows anything but them, especially when they work among people who can't make the kind of showing they do. I am afraid it will be a long time before the Negro outgrows this condition of immature thinking, and the pitiful thing about it is instead of being helpful, many of them suck the very life blood out of the people they pretend to help. Of course, all are not like that, but far too many are."

That night Eve dreamed of all the beauty of her childhood days. She skipped rope at the little one-room schoolhouse of long, long ago. She went around the country side gathering the children who didn't go to church and each Saturday after their work was done, she had a Bible class with them. She played around the old gin house, waiting for Paw Vest to have his cotton ginned. She wrote love letters in the sand and picked huckleberries for sale; went to the store to get a plug of brown mule tobacco for Paw Vest; heard Maw Jenny praying as she passed the door of the little house in the Lems' yard. Then she heard her begin her usual hymn.

Oh! it was a wonderful dream. She tried to remain there on the Lems' plantation and join the field hands in their song fest, their melon feast, their yearly picnic. Then she and a group she called her buddies would discuss to themselves what each wanted to do when they grew up. Eve always wanted to be a teacher and have a husband and a baby. Sammylee, Eve's closest friend, wanted a husband who would not make her pick cotton and pull fodder like her daddy did. She also wanted a little girl who would look just like her friend Eve.

She and Sammylee ran in the woods and gathered flowers of all kinds. They found some honeysuckle and ate them. How great it seemed in this dream to be young again; to listen to the hoot of the owl and throw salt in the fire to stop him from hooting; to see all the oldsters at the yearly farm picnic giving the young people a sample of the square dance they did when they were young. Then off to Uncle Jim's house they would run to hear the only phonograph they ever had seen. How they laughed when the record played was "Pray for the Lights To Go Out." How she learned the words and Maw Lou heard her one day singing:

> My father was a deacon
> In the First Baptist Church
> Way down south where
> I was born.

80

People used to come from
Miles around just to
See the holy work go on.
One old sister she got
Happy, she shimmyed,
She wobbled and
Then she balled the jack.
She hollered, brother!
If you want to spread
Joy, pray for the lights
To go out.

What a dressing down she got from both Maw
Lou, her mother, and Maw Jenny. She would never
sing that again. They told her it was plumb wicked
and Eve didn't want to do anything wicked; as when
she and her brother Sonny put bags on their feet
to go to Paw Vest's watermelon patch to keep him
from seeing their tracks. Then one day later in the
afternoon just as she was in the melon patch thump-
ing the big, ripe melons, Paw Vest walked out from
a corn field that surrounded the melon patch and
asked her if she wanted a melon. She was stunned
and said no, but he told her to take the one she had
thumped. Then he went home with her, told her to
cut it. Then he sat down and ordered her to eat it.
She ate till her eyes nearly popped out, but Paw Vest
would not let her stop until he was satisfied of her
punishment. She often laughed and said she never
went near that watermelon patch again. "Oh, I had
much rather have been whipped with his belt," she
often said. She woke up running from the dog in Mr.
Lems' yard. When she told Bill her dream, he
laughed and said "that means we must visit the old
plantation tomorrow."

On their trip through the Pee Dee Section the view

81

was a real reminder of the past. She passed the creek where the old-fashioned car got tucked in the soft sand around the creek bank on her first trip out looking for a job as a "school mam." Old Preacher Coleman, who was driving the car, had to spend the night in it. Eve had gotten out when dark came on and tried walking through the swamp to find help. She nearly died from sheer exhaustion through the storm and wind that was raging that night. They passed the old tobacco barn where she had banded and strung tobacco under its cool shed during World War I. She was a very young girl then and never dreamed that she would one day come back to these scenes and wish with all her heart she could live them again. She saw new and strange faces working under the old log and adobe clay barn, but they reminded her of all the happiness she once knew on the Lems plantation. How she would run at noon each day to meet the mail man who drove a gray horse hitched to a rubber-tired buggy. Every time he had a letter for her he would blow his whistle. She grew up seeing that mail carrier every day in that community and it seemed like he had to be there now in his buggy with the pleasant smile that he always wore.

Even Maw Jenny loved Mr. Gray, the mail carrier. One day when Sis, Maw Jenny's oldest daughter, had sent her a box, Maw Jenny asked Mr. Gray to cut the cords on the box for her. As he looked on, Maw Jenny took the two pair of long drawers out the box, holding them in her hand while Mr. Gray drove away laughing in spite of himself. Eve could feel the warmth and friendship that had existed in that community all through the long, long years. She wished, as they rode along, sometimes stopping to

82

chat with old friends, that it was huckleberry time again and that she could get her ten-pound lard bucket and join the happy, merry singing group of huckleberry pickers as they swarmed the woods to pick berries during the noon hour.

She could see the face of Maw Lou light up with a big smile when she saw that Eve had picked her bucket full. Maw Lou would can some for her family and the Lems family. She would never think of canning for herself without plans to can some for Mrs. Lems, too. That had always been a rule in her house. Even Paw Vest, who loved to make wine from the plums, peaches, green corn and blackberries, always made enough for Mr. Lems and his friends. They always looked forward to serving Paw Vest's wine to entertain at Christmas time.

Bill stopped to talk with Sam, who had been working the North for a few months. "Heard you were north, working. Didn't expect to see you," Bill said.

"Me, man, I jest got plumb tired beating my shadow out to work in de morning and when I got home in de evening while I opening de do', look back and see my shadow puffing and blowing and coming up the steps 'hind me. Fess, I tell you I wouldn't gone up da in the firse place. I had a good job here in de garbage truck, but where I went, dat's a white man's job. I did git a job helping where my brother worked in de kitchen at de hospital. I see him drive down here in he fine car. I figgered he was 'living it up,' but man he hardly knows what his own house looks lake. Dat man and his wife run to work eber day like a pack of hounds. I much ruther be here. See, me sitting under dis tree. I done my work fur der day and man, ain't I just cooling out. Den dey have de nerve tu talk about 'down South.' Man, I wouldn't swap places wid dem fur all de money in de world. Most uf dem work all de time and can't vite you in to eat a meal. If you there at eating time. dey hide and eat tu keep from offering you any. Some uf dem dey eat one at a time where I lived. I am poor, me and Sally, but since I stopped drinking and cided to live right, us jest doing all right fur us selves. Den Mr. Mc-Swain here is good to his workers. Sally gets lots ub help fur du chilun like clothes and due lack from du house where she works. Even help out wid de victuals. I plan soon to buy us a little house so us can really call the place us live home."

Bill interrupted: "Yes, Sam, I think that's the thing to do. You have a nice large family. Soon you will have children in high school and then college. So a nice home for them will surely be in order," Bill concluded.

Just as they started to drive away, Sam hollered: "Wait, Fess. I got some watermelons I want you tu have." He went in the house and came out grinning with two big melons, one under each arm. "Dis is what I tell you about here in du South, and, too, you ought to see my pigs and chickens. Wish you and Miss Eve would come back Sunday fur dinner. I know Sally would love dat."

Bill and Eve thanked Sam and assured him they would come back soon, but could not give a definite date since both were quite busy doing the survey Bill had undertaken among his people.

After leaving and having talked with Sam, Bill could readily see there had been a change in Sam's thinking. He knew that the world in which we live is controlled by thought. He said to Eve as they rode through this beautiful country side together: "You know the man or woman who thinks best is the man

84

or woman who gets the most out of life. Of course, I find many people among those I meet who will ask me, 'What is the use of spending the time to develop myself, my children or to contribute to the development of my neighbor's children when all that it will amount to is our being thrown into a war and perhaps destroyed?'"

"Yes," Eve said. "I know there are people who think like that. It is the people who assume this attitude toward life in the world in which who hinder progress and delay the winning of the cold war in which we are engaged," Eve went on as Bill drove slowly along a dirt road that led to the very spot on which had sat the little one-room school where each had learned their ABC's. He could hear the old-time teacher, Miss Ollie, drilling them until they knew them thoroughly from memory. Sometimes she would slip up behind him while he was looking back and cut him across the back with her hickory switch. It would sting like a bee and he would be afraid to tell his parents about it lest he get another whipping worse than that.

He remembered his first reading lesson. It was about some biddies and an old hen. Because he saw one wandering away he decided within himself that the chicks were disobeying. He did not know a word in the reading. So when Uncle Frank, a stern old preacher, who had succeeded Miss Ollie, told him to read, he started expressing his own ideas: "Oh, little biddy, little biddy, why didn't you mind your mammy?" The old teacher, realizing that Bill didn't know a word in his lesson, picked up his hickory and came across Bill's back, saying: "Oh, little Billy, little Billy, why didn't you learn your lesson?" From that day until Bill left the community to live with an uncle after the death of his father, he never went into Uncle Frank's class without his lessons. He never forgot or quite forgave him for the marks left across his back. He often told the story and said he was glad that punishing children in school like that had been abolished.

Eve laughed, too, as he related it this day while driving through that community. She teased Bill for holding a grudge. Just then they passed the little Shady Grove Church. It still looked the same except for a brand new coat of paint and the loss of a number of trees that used to serve as hitching posts for the horses. Eve kind of wished, as they rode by that she could have just gotten one glimpse of Paw Vest getting out of the buggy, and after helping Maw out, getting all the kids out the front and back. She could see the little dangling feet and stiff white collars of Sunny and Bun as they made their way to the "House of God" each Sunday to learn how to live a life of service to God and man that Paw Vest "would teach them." She could see Aunt Ellen shouting with buttons of all colors flying in all directions, out of the pocket she wore under her skirt, along with tobacco and an old cob pipe, not to mention a few scented dried ginger and caramel roots that she carried along to "sweeten the breath."

They got out and walked around and discovered that weeds had overgrown the little country path behind the church that let out into the woods where the members went to see about themselves since there were no toilet facilities anywhere except the few houses around that had outdoor toilets.

"My, how things have changed here. They have a pool in the church, outdoor toilets, lights and just to think how happy we were here with kerosene

86

lamps and feeling for each other in the dark when we had night service."

Bill, who had not spoken since they found this little path, spoke: "You can see what progress does for a place and its people. You see in every walk of life leadership is needed and leadership does not fall into one's hands unless one is prepared for its responsibilities, and if by accident it does fall into one's hands who is ill prepared for it, the more miserable will his failure be."

"Yes, Bill, I get it. The better leadership we have the more progress our people will make even during this racial crisis. We need leaders with the Spirit of Christ, who are full of humility and filled with a love for service rather than a love of self," Eve said.

On their way back to the car, Eve peeped through the little church windows. There was the same stage on which she had recited her first little speech. "I remember it so well, Bill. I was only four years old and Maw Jenny had drilled me for weeks.

"Two little eyes to look to God,
Two little ears to hear his word,
Two little hands to do his will
One little tongue to sing His praise."

Eve stopped there for over in the corner of the church were the chair seats where Paw Vest used to sit and sing. She seemed to hear his high tenor voice and see him smiling as he sat there and sang with all his heart, "Rock of Ages, cleft for me, let me hide myself in Thee," and then in a lower tone she heard him singing:

"Amazing Grace, how sweet the sound,
That saved a wretch like me.
I once was lost but now I'm found,
Was blind but now I see."

Bill looked at Eve. There were tears in her eyes as he led her away toward the car.

"Stop a minute, wait," Eve said as she turned and started up the path that led to her Uncle Jim's house. Yes, opposite the little white church, Uncle Jim's house sat among a grove of trees and flowers. He was one of her precious links which reminded her of good times of the past. He was always so full of the zeal for living that some of it was imparted to all whom he chanced to meet. You could hear him laughing all over that little community. "Ha, ha, ha ha! I be dog it it ain't good to see you," or "I ain't seen you in coon days. Cume on in and have a set down. Pull your chair up tu the table and stick your feet under and have a bit." Then he would begin telling a story that would keep all laughing. Sometimes it was about his courting. "Ha, ha, ha! I learn long ago never to eedrop."

"How, Uncle Jim?" Eve would ask.

"Well, when I was a young man I hurd another fellow was going wid my best gal. So one Sunday night when I drove in sight ub her house and saw his horse hitched tu the hitching post, I decided to creep up tu the house, crawl under it and peep up through the big crack in the floor and watch and listen to what they had to say. Well, they talked bout me until it was all I could do to keep them from knowing I was there. The gal laughed about my big feet, even said I wore my breeches too tight, but worst of all she said I was plum ugly and never combed my hair. Man, wasn't I hot! Why, I crawled out from there and neber went near that house again. From dat day on I never eedropped."

Then he would tell about his two nieces trying to teach him: "Why us was in the cafe up town and I

said if it don't rain Chuesday I am going a fishing.
Truddy, who had been to college, whispered to me:
'Uncle Jim, don't say Chuesday. It's Tuesday.' But
I shut her up. I tell her 'Here you is, ain't got the
milk off your mouth trying to teach me. It been
Cheusday when I wus born and hit go be Chuesday
when I die.' "

Eve would agree for she had learned long ago that
a child couldn't teach Uncle Jim, and all were children if they were young.

She and Bill walked up the path to the house. Eve
knew she would never hear him joke again nor see
the big, broad grin on his face that just made one
feel at home without words. Her heart was heavy
and her big, brow eyes were cloudy. Bill knew how
much she had loved Uncle Jim. He came next to Paw
Vest with her, she always said. So Bill stopped,
begged her to turn around before they got to the
house, for he knew her going there would bring back
memories she couldn't forget.

Yes, like the time Uncle Jim made a bet and raced
with his neighbor's horse and won. That was a feat
he often laughed about and told how he nearly fainted at the end of the road. Then there was a time
when he and his Indian Daddy had run three hundred people away from a school program when a
fight began. When he Daddy wrung off a tree top in
the school yard and started waving it and saying to
those who were fighting Uncle Jim, "Damit. If my
son go to hell, I am gwine long wid him." People began running, leaving him and his father in full pos-
session of the schoolground. Eve knew Grandpa was
nearly seven feet, and Uncle Jim was six or more, so
in those days they must have looked like giants in
that small community. No one ever knew Grandpa

89

but his family and the business men with whom he had dealings, for when he wasn't hunting and fishing or visiting with some of the married children, he was at home. He never visited outsiders, never spoke to anyone who mistreated him.

Maw Lou told her that he used to go to church, but one day when he was fishing, he saw some of the deacons taking fish from his nets when they didn't know he was around. He never went back to church or spoke to those deacons. That was when Maw Lou was a small child. Although he didn't go to church, he let Maw Jenny go and take the children every Sunday. Even bought a surrey with the fringe on top for them to ride in.

Then when he got down sick, two of the old deacons who were still living came to see him and ask forgiveness. It was too late. He didn't recognize them. Then his children came, some of whom he hadn't spoken to in years because they married without his consent after he had refused their request. He lay there a week, just looking into space. Late on Friday evening while Maw Lou, his daughter, was mopping his face and sopping his mouth with water to keep its moisture, he said: "God knows, I love children. I used to make like I didn't. God knows I love them." With these words he closed his eyes and fell asleep.

The funeral was on Sunday. For the first time in fifty years or more the whole family went to church together. Eve recalled how his son Mack came home just as they returned from the funeral. How angry he was because they didn't wait for him. No member of the family or friends could reason with him.

He left and promised never to come again and he didn't. Maw Jenny just smiled and sang, and when anyone discussed him, she would say: "He chip off de old block, don fly far."

CHAPTER X

Twilight in the Southern Sky

WHEN Eve and Bill got back home, it was late and they were very tired, yet they could not retire after supper until they had discussed all the happenings during the day's visit to the little Shady Grove community.

"Oh! I don't mean to be a sentimentalist, but when I visit the old plantation, I feel like I have left something very important behind me. After we get here to Warrenville, I am happy for days it seems," Eve said, looking at Bill and studying the serious expression on his face.

Finally she spoke: "Well, I can understand why the people we met today were so cordial, both white and Negroes, not to mention your Uncle Jim's children. When we took the wrong road and went around that place you called 'Circle End' and got lost from the highway, well, who would have thought that white man who lived in that beautiful home and was playing tennis on his own court would have stopped and gone in his house, found the place we wanted to go on the map, then got in his car and led the way to the highway for us. I can never thank him enough for I was really lost. I tell you the South has some of the kindest people anywhere in the world, I believe, and I have been abroad and visited many places; but for kindness and consideration, the

92

South tops them all. Notwithstanding we have lots to improve here, but with hard work and sympathetic understanding among our people the right improvement will be made in time. I sincerely believe we should strive to win admiration as people, not try to demand what we want by fighting for 'our rights.' No one will stand to be ordered around too much and especially by a people which on the whole has so little in an economical sense to offer."

Eve sat listening as Bill concluded: "I was impressed the other day when we took Jane to see about that job. While you and the lady were talking, I was listening. I heard her tell you about Aunt Mary who was working for them."

"Oh, yes, Bill," Eve continued. "She said Aunt Mary had been there thirty years and had reared both of their children. Now, she was old and could not do hard work but Mrs. Copps says she can't do without her, pays her to come and talk to them. She stated also that Aunt Mary was like a member of the family."

"Yes, honey. I thought that real interesting and was listening attentively while you both talked. Now, I believe we have had a full day and the 'Old Professor' is tired. I mean, Eve, honey, I am really tired."

He was yawning now and Eve decided that they had had enough for one day.

After Bill had retired that night, he lay thinking of a statement he had read in the history of Negro soldiers in the Spanish-American War. "We are coming, boys. It's a little slow and tiresome but we are coming." He said to Eve next morning as they sat at the table eating breakfast: "You know, honey, I have come to the conclusion that the solution of the

93

Negro problem is mainly in his own hands. One thing he needs most in the South is equal protection by the law. No one can keep him down but himself."

Eve sighed and asked, "Bill, aren't you treading on dangerous grounds?"

"Yes, I guess I will be hung in effigy when I report my findings relative to this survey I have just completed, but I have encased myself in several metal hides, hence I can stand the 'rips' when they are made. If a man wants to do a real service for his fellowmen, he must be prepared for criticisms and accept them. People have a right to express their likes and dislikes, and that is one freedom that helps make America great. Your school begins next week and I have a feeling that I have almost climbed to the top of life's hills. I couldn't have done so without you, darling; and now the 'Old Fessor' has got to go over to the other side."

There were tears in Eve's eyes and they fell on her high cheek bones. She had noticed Bill slowing up for sometime. She had seen him working all summer, gathering information about his people as if each day was the last. She knew Bill had served the people of Warrenville for forty years. He loved those people because he had seen them grow from infancy to full maturity. He came there when the town had all outdoor toilets. Many times he had stopped the boys from laughing at the "privy man" as he loaded and drove through the town with his obnoxious load. He had seen the Negroes, many working from "scratch" who had become home- and landowners. He had worked with the citizens, both whites and Negroes, for better relationship and improvement. Through his effort dark streets were lighted, dirt streets were paved. Traffic lights in Negro districts

94

improved; school- and playgrounds were second to none. He always said when people talked about the Negro problem that the Negro was his own problem to a great degree. "I have had experience here with the leaders of Warrenville and I find that Negroes don't get lots of things because they never ask and seem satisfied. I admit there are areas to approach and correct conditions in those areas. This can be done when leaders of both races work together for the benefit of the whole."

"Bill, you are not a fighting man, are you?" Eve asked.

After some thought, Bill replied: "No, I have been through two wars and I wonder if fighting ever accomplishes the purposes for which it was intended. Some times I think it brings about more hate and complicated problems than can ever be settled. I believe that reasoning among leaders across tables will in the end be more beneficial. Of course, the exceptions are always there."

"Then, what?" Eve asked, smiling.

"Just get together and get rid of it."

"Oh, I see you do not believe to a limited degree in a fight."

"Well, I mean if you got a fellow acting up, either set him down or get rid of him."

The summer passed and school in Warrenville began with its usual crowd and responsibilities. Bill had worked with the people of this community and understood their problems. One of the immediate needs was more recreational facilities. Those were being met and everyone was proud of their community and was working to improve it.

The fall was warm with an Indian-like summer. On weekends, Bill and Eve would drive out into the

95

country from which came many of the pupils since Warrenville High was the only high school in that area. One Friday they stopped in to see Aunt Molly. She didn't get out but managed to keep up with all the news in the community. They hadn't been seated long before she began to realate to them the latest. long before she began to relate to them the latest. school. Well, her mammy let her go north in der summer to work and de wost thing happen dat I eber hurd happen tu a poor gurl."

"What was it?" Eve asked.

"Why, you know her old daddy left her Maw Lou when Leda was a baby. Well, wait now you ain't hurd der half."

Eve and Bill were seated on the edge of their chairs, waiting to hear the rest of her story for Aunt Molly always told the most interesting things they had ever heard, like the old lady Chusy, who used to sing in the cabin by the branch. Eve could never forget the words of this touching song and the story Aunt Molly told about it. Eve often found herself humming and picturing the old slave woman singing:

"You is de one little ting I love,
So hush-a-by in de old log cabin,
And cross old Chilly and de stars above.
Years will come and go in de old log cabin
You will grow up big, my baby,
And den der'll be no cross old Chilly,
For to rock you den, my baby,
But when de stars eber shining on de cabin,
Will you tink of me den once more.
Oh, will you remember de old log cabin,
And cross old Chilly and de cabin door.
Hush-a-by, my little pickaninny,

You de one little thing I love.
Hush up, my little one, hush up, my sugar one,
Hush up, my sweetheart dear."

There were always tears in Eve's eyes when she
sang it, for as the story goes, Aunt Chilly and the
baby got burned up in "de cabin" and Aunt Molly
claimed that, late in the evening on a rainy day, she
could still be heard rocking and singing to her baby
down by the old moss-grown creek. So Eve was satisfied to listen when Aunt Molly, who with her remarkable memory and keen wit, told of the bygone
days.

"Yes," Aunt Molly continued. "Well, she met uh
man up here whare she worked. Oh! she wrote Lou
a-telling her how good looking he was. Said he had
black, curly hair, wid a silver lock in the front. Well,
Lou neber thought much about hit 'cause eber time
she write her Maw she was sending her money and
telling what a good job she had, and how nice hur
Ainty wus to her. Lou kinder hoped she'd git a good
husband and not end up like her."

"What really happened?" Eve interrupted.

"Why, last week der gal cum home to git ready
fur de wedding. Hur Maw had planned hit at der
church. Chuesday morning at der table she brought
her Mammy der picture uf de man, and what you
reckin?"

"What?" Bill and Eve asked in unison.

"Why, the good fur nothing, stinking rascal was
the gal own daddy dat left Lou when der child was
a baby."

"Great June!" Eve uttered and remembered that
was her pet word in school. Bill shook his head and
got up and began to pace the floor while the old lady

97

finished. "Now wait. Lou fainted. The gal is in some secret hideout dey say. I dunno. Der last time I saw dem the doctor and der preacher was dare, and I tell you if dey eber needed dem, dey show do need dem now," Aunt Molly concluded, to which Bill and Eve agreed.

"I tell you dis hear place has had a share of everything. I just trust in de Lord 'cause I know He been good to me and He neber put more on a body dan he can bear. Sue'll get over it and der next time she fall in love I bet she gwine know who der man be 'fore she gage herself to him, I bet," she finished with a sad note.

Bill and Eve always ate supper when they went to Aunt Molly's because her granddaughters thought "the world" of "Professor Bill" and "Miss Eve." While they were sitting on the porch, her great-grandson Peter came from the barn, carrying a big, dead rat he had caught in the barn.

"What are you to do with it?" Bill asked Peter as her passed the side porch.

"Maw gwine fry fur Sis. She pees her bed," the little seven-year-old boy replied.

Well, that was a new one for bed-wetting, Bill and Eve thought as they watched from the porch as the boy skinned and cleaned the rat. Now, Eve wondered as she went to supper! She knew everything was clean for she had eaten there since early chilhood, but the idea of the rat being cooked made her stomach churn.

After leaving there, it was just around the bend where Uncle Simon lived. They would be sure to stop, for he was getting feeble. He was so glad to see them and Eve was equally glad to see him. She called him and Aunt Molly links with a glorious past.

He had just got in the wood and started a little fire in the fireplace; he felt chilly he told Bill, and his rheumatism was bothering him again. While they were there, Sam came by to see his daddy. He was as jovial and happy-go-lucky as ever. He told about a talk he and his boss had about segregation. "I tell him if he answer my question, then I can answer his."

"What was your question?" Bill finally asked.

"I say, if I got a pig and you take 'em, den you have a hog, and if I take him is I taking your hog or is I taking my pig?"

"What did he say?" Bill asked.

"He laughed and shake his head."

"Well, you have brought up the race issue again, Sam. In our quest for justice, let us forget about the past injustices in bracing ourselves for the conflict. Remember, this is not a military war. It will depend largely on the way the Negro deports himself."

Bill knew that if the American Negro ever came into his own as a race, it would not be by raking up past injustices and past cruelties inflicted upon his people. They must climb up themselves with such assistance as they can get from their white friends. Time, which some refuse to take into account, will be the greatest adjuster of their problems. Bill told Sam, "We must be like Paul, who wrote: 'Forgetting those things which are behind, we press forward to work for the high calling which is in Christ Jesus. That can be applied in our case, so let us go forth with love for all and malice toward none."

Sam sat for a minute with his hands under his chin. Then he said, "Reckin you right, Fesser. Us doing good here now. In fact, since I can member us neber had hit so good before. Sometimes I git bum-

99

fuddled when some uf dese people come here tu speak us about us rights. I believe hit leaves most of us bumfuddle. Oh! I ain't tell you bout Pete little boy Tug."

"What happened?" was Eve's quick response, seeing the sad expression on Sam's face.

"Well, dere is a old pond back uf de house in de woods, and last week him and two outher boys wandered off from de house, playing, and went tu de pond. Pete and his ole lady had wen tu town to sell some bacco. When they got back, dey couldn't find Tug nowhare in der neighborhood. Den dey found out he and Denny Smith little boys was playing tugether. Well, dey got hold uf dese boys. At fust dey say dey ain't know where Tug is. Den de little bit a fellow started crying and tell 'em Tug in pond. Oh! hit was de saddest thing eber happened in dis here community. Look like Pete old lady gwine crazy. Dat was dare only child."

"Oh, we are so sorry to hear that. When did it happen?" Eve asked as Bill sat silent. "We might stop by on our way home. I taught his mother when she was in the grades," Eve recalled.

On their way home Eve and Bill talked about the different things learned on a trip to the old plantation.

"Yes, that big plantation is a world within a world. You hear good news here, bad news over there, humorous news across the creek and see funny things along the road, but when an innocent seven-year-old boy gets drowned in some old good-for-nothing pond that no one uses, it's something that pulls at your heartstrings. Just think of that poor mother! I tell you, there should be more recreational places in the rural areas for all children. I mean safe places to play," Bill asserted.

Eve didn't speak. She was a mother and the expression on her face told the story of a mother's heart. That would be one place they were compelled to go.

When they arrived, they found Tug's mother in bed. Her husband explained to them that she had refused food for several days and he was calling in a doctor. Bill asked him if he had not decided on a special doctor, to call in "Little Bud," our own doctor. But Pete thanked him and told him, "We never call a doctor on this place. We go up to the 'House' and tell the boss and the doctor, he here in little or 'no time."

Bill remembered that when he was young the people on the plantation never worried about getting a doctor. He thought they had long since stopped that but he was mistaken. Some still depend on the landlord to look after their physical needs.

Bill told Eve after they had been shown Tug's little "shed room" on the porch where he kept his little fishing pole on a rack beside the wall, a coonskin cap his father Pete had given him; also his two pairs of shoes, a "Sunday-go-to-meeting" pair his mother called them, and an everyday par. There were little drawings of frogs and pigs and horses tacked on the wall, all the work of little Tug's hands. On the head of his wooden bed was posted his Sunday school cards. His parents told Bill and Eve how much he enjoyed going to Sunday school.

"The Sunday before he drowned he recited his Bible verse: Suffer little children to come unto Me and forbid them not for of such is the Kingdom of Heaven," his mother said with tears in her eyes.

Then she held up a pair of little blue overalls with patches on each knee and tearfully she told them, "These are the last little breeches he wore."

Pete finished the story: "These are the ones he drowned in. His mother insisted on keeping them as a reminder, I reckin. I wish she wouldn't. She stays in this room most of the time. I told her this thing will drive her mad if it keeps up."

Bill and Eve tried to console her and asked her to try and go away for a while to forget, a thing they themselves didn't believe. Bill and Eve didn't speak for a long time on their way home. When they did, Eve suggested they go by Rev. Eli's and explain the situation as they had found it at Pete's house, since they were members of his church. They felt a visit from Rev. Eli would help both Pete and his wife to see their loss in its true perspective.

The school year passed swiftly, with the usual race-problem discussions at each meeting. One night after one of these meetings, Bill told the audience that the Negroes' problem in American was not a race problem. It was an economic problem, and if the local Negroes in each section would make an all-out effort to solve it by conferring with the local white people of each section and seeking a workable solution, it could be done quicker and on more friendly terms than is being done by so much national political fanfare.

"The relationship all over the country would be better if we set ourselves sincerely to the gigantic task before us. It would lessen the rioting among our people that is now occurring in the larger cities because of the big-mouthed, self-seeking politicians. for what he needs than for what he wants. He rec- The Negro must be taught to spend his money more

102

ognizes his needs along many lines and one is to teach his people how to use the ballot properly. An ignorant use of a good tool can be harmful. Yes, voting is a citizen's right; therefore, he should learn the responsibilities that go with that privilege. He should know the people for whom he votes, and not be like one of my patrons who told me at the booth when I asked him for whom he was voting, he said, 'Any uf 'em will do, none uf dem mean me nuthing.' Now, friends, you can't get something for nothing. So let us as Negroes be sure that we have done our part and that we do our part in brightening the corner where we are."

Bill sat down. The patrons applauded. Little did they know at that last meeting of the year that the Old Professor had made his last talk to the P.T.A. He had told them many times about having faith like "our fathers had," a real, living, working faith in God.

That June, when commencement came, the Old Professor was ill, but he'd not given up. He told his students that they would have to win their place in the world on their own merit. "You can't sit around complaining about what has been done to your people unless you have a great knowledge of history and know upon whom to place the blame. That blame does not rest wholly upon the South, but upon the people who, after the Civil War, put unqualified Negroes in positions formerly held by trained whites. The Negroes just out of slavery had no inkling of how to run a government or a town. What a subtle way to help a man knowing he couldn't hold out. As a result, there sprang up hate groups that killed and molested Negroes. Now, can you tell who really was to blame? There are many angles to consider before

103

you point an accusing finger at a given section, although no one is justified in wrongdoing. So I say to you go forth, learn to think for yourselves. Find the truth. The only way to learn truth or facts is to seek for it. In closing, I would like to say to this class: whatsoever things are lovely, whatsoever things are just, whatsoever things are pure, whatsoever things are of good report, if there be any virture, if there be any praise, think on these things."

Bill couldn't stop there. He continued. "The world is getting smaller but thank God that the people in the world are getting bigger all the time, and you will have to continually grow if you want a place alongside the people who have already grown big and are still growing. They will accept you only as you grow. You are American citizens. Make your contributions so great that America will not see you as a Negro, but an American helping America to be and remain the greatest nation on earth." With this, the "Old Professor" sat down. He had come to the end of his journey.

Next day at home several of the patrons called on him. Some of his students who graduated the night before came to see him and bid him goodbye since they were going into the Army or away to work. Eve was glad school had ended for she and Bill could now have some time of their own. She knew Warrenville, and as long as they remained home they belonged to the people. There would be little privacy, so she begged Bill to leave for a rest. They would visit Helen in Los Angeles.

The following day they packed and boarded the train for California. "Little Bud," the doctor, was against Bill's taking the trip, but gave in after Bill promised to take it easy.

104

When they reached California, Eve could see Bill was a sick man. A doctor was called in and Bill was put to bed. For a week Eve did nothing but nurse her ailing husband. Then one day, while she was opening the blinds, he looked out and said with a smile: "Eve, darling, please take me back South to our home in Warrenville where we have been so happy."

Eve couldn't turn around to answer for the tears were blinding her eyes. Her Bill was weakening. Her Bill, her Bill on whom her whole life centered. She turned and went to him, put her head down and kissed his fevered brow. "Yes, darling, I will take you home if you want to go. Let me get in touch with the doctor."

Bill tried to smile as he said: " 'Little Bud' advised me against this trip. He was right. It was too much after a hard year's work. You know we spent the summer making the survey, and then right into the schoolhouse. Guess I am all beaten," he concluded with a sigh.

Helen did not want to hear of them leaving. "Why, we have some of the best doctors in the world here," she assured them.

"Yes, Helen, but Bill says he appreciates all you have done and are doing. He just wants to go home and I would hate to keep him here if he grows worse and I couldn't take him home."

Helen saw Eve's point and soon arrangements were made for him to travel home in comfort. There he could sit upstairs in his room by the window and look down on the street below. Could see his own grocery store across the street, the funeral parlor that he had owned for years. There on the other side of the street was the corner drug store owned by

105

"Little Bud," now Warrenville's only Negro doctor.

There was the little row of white houses with their neat, trimmed lawns and beautiful flowers, together with the friendly faces of their owners who always greeted him with a smile.

It was not long after being home that he began to mend and for a while Eve thought he would get well.

"It seems to help him so much to be here with the people he knows and loves," Eve told the doctor one day. "Oh! how he enjoys telling his grandsons about Warrenville and its conditions when he was a boy. How the people lived, comparing them with our present living standards. You know Mike and Butch are to take over the business under my supervision, of course," Eve continued as she expressed her surprise to the doctor about Bill's sudden change in his attitude toward many things. Little did she know that Bill was preparing for a long trip over the mountains of life down into the beautiful paradise valley of peace.

Some days he felt well enough to walk with his stick down to the corner drug store and chat with the town folks who were always glad to see him.

Late one evening in the fall he told Eve he wanted to visit the school and other places he hadn't seen since he returned from California. Uncle Simon was one of his favorite characters. It was he who Bill said had so much plain horse sense that one didn't find in books. He always said he learned something new every time he visited Aunt Molly or Uncle Simon.

Today Bill seemed so happy, visiting these two friends who were two of the oldest people around those parts.

106

Aunt Molly put her arms around his neck. "Fessor, I hurd you wus sick and I tried tu get der children tu bring me tu see you cause you one uf us boys. I knowed you Mammy and you Pappy. So glad to see you up and about again. I stayed on my knees asking God to spare you fur der good you done around dis here place and here you is able tu come and see me." With those words the old lady said, "Thank God. He answers prayers.

Bill assured her he appreciated her interest and after staying there a while Eve drove to Uncle Simon's. He was out in the yard, cutting up some stove wood when he saw them. "Be dog, if hit ain't 'Fessor.' Gladdest in de world to see you. I plan to get on my mule back and go to town Saday. You know my old wagon wheel done wore out and I ain't been able to buy anuther yet. My son Bob said he he would take me in his car but I ruther ride old Dan. You know they always say: 'Slow but steady wins de race.' I jest like driving my ole mule Dan."

Yes. Eve and Bill knew Uncle Simon was one of the old-timers who still drove to Warrenville and hitched their stock to the old remaining hitching post. He would never change. He belonged completely to a wonderful past.

During the following weeks Bill grew worse. The doctor told Eve it was just a matter of time. Long years of hard work had taken its toll. Yes, his heart was failing under the strain.

Bill seemed to derive a peculiar pleasure sitting by his window, listening to the early-rising green-peas-and-butterbeans salesladies, some with bags of beans on head and measuring cup in hand. You could hear them call out: "Green P-e-a-s! and b-u-t-t-e-r-b-e-a-n-s!" Sometimes a small child with them would repeat the same sentence. Bill did not seem worried. He possessed the attitude of a man who had finished his work.

CHAPTER XI

Deep Are the Roots

WHEN the new recreation building was completed, it was named in honor of Bill, the first principal of Warrenville High School. It had been nearly a year since he was forced to retire because of ill health. Most of the people, especially the older ones, thought of him as head of Warrenville High, but it had been months since he was able to attend any of its programs.

Each day sitting by the window and looking out over the little town brought back memories of old. Yes, like most people who have reached old age with its cruel outlook, the grave, he too began to look back to youth; yes, youth, the "good old days." Bill thought of the times when he was a small boy riding in the back seat of his father's wagons with his feet dangling out. The time he crossed over a twenty-foot-deep hole of water on a log after trying to walk it and getting scared. How when he had got over to the other side of the creek, he was greeted by a big blacksnake that nearly took what little breath he had left after the crossing. How he ran to his granddaddy's house which was nearby and got a hoe to kill the snake. The time he saw a small alligator in the swamp where a number of his daddy's hogs had been missed from the pasture. The children's annual picnics, the old folks' square dance where his granddaddy would jump up and clap his feet together three times before touching the floor, a feat few young people could perform at that time. He could see the place where the old lamplighter used to stop and light his lamp on the newly painted lamppost. Of all the girls and boys with whom he played and jumped ditches, most of them had gone to the beautiful valley of peace.

Then he would face reality and whisper to himself: "Times like those will be no more." Brave as he was, his brows clouded and he fell victim to human weakness as he held the tear drops on his cheeks.

One day as Bill sat lonely, he heard someone coming up the stairway, walking with a stick. He turned to meet the dusky, wrinkled but smiling face of Aunt Molly.

"Well, Eve tell me tu cum on up cause you know I 'homefolks.' Jest had to cum see you tuday. I dreamed bout you last night so I tell Liz dis marning you gwine take me tu see 'Fessor,' dis verry day. So here I cum." With this remark she reached for Bill's hands: "How you feeling, honey? You look better dan you did last time I seen you. Show glad tu see you looking better."

Bill directed her to a chair, and she began to relate all the plantation's happenings as usual.

"You know Brudder Simon sick? Dat's why he ain't been here dis week. Hit rained and his rheumatism cum back on him. You know he neber go tu a doctor. Why, when you axed him about going to de doctor, he tell you de doctor don't cure hisself. So he send 'Pug,' his grandson, down tu de creek to git some of du mud off de bank dat look like silver. Den

110

he makes a poultice and wrapped hit around his joints dat hurt him. He allus git up after den."

"Well, how is he this morning?" Bill asked, trying to get in a word.

"Simon gitting along all right. Hit's Pug dat sick."

"What's troubling him?"

"Why, a snake bit him while he was on du bank. He put his foot under an old stump and du snake was da and bit him. Dey brung him to the doctor and he better now. Simon say he oughta went hisself because he knows eber habit and trick uf a devilish old snake."

Aunt Molly finished her story and went downstairs to talk with Eve before time for her grandson to pick her up and take her back to the old plantation.

"Eve, I don't see how in de world you kin climb dem steps to bout Fessor. Den you sleep up dare. Why, I would be so tired when I climb up da and fall in bed, dat if Gabriel blowed his trumpet I wouldn't hear unless he cum up dere and shake me."

Eve laughed and assured Aunt Molly that she never gave climbing those stairs a thought. She was so accustomed to them.

Then with fond memory recalling the past, she told her that Bill had that house built just for her. It was a wedding present. How she loved the blue and pink bedrooms upstairs. "Yes, Bill and I chose the blue one and Ruthie the pink one. We have never lived anywhere else since moving here, as you know, many, many years ago. We have grown and changed with Warrenville. I have tried to get Bill to come down here in one of the downstairs rooms but he won't. Up there holds so many pleasant memories for him, he says."

After dinner Aunt Molly left. "Reckin I done all de harm I kin. I got to go now, but I'll be back soon. Tell Fessor I gone cause I don want to wake him, and be show and take good care uf dat boy."

Eve got Aun Molly's walking stick and helped her find her old cob pipe. She had forgotten where she put it on a small cabinet in the kitchen.

It was always nice to have Aunt Molly, Eve thought. She was a reminder of her childhood days on the old plantation, and she had not changed one bit with the modern times.

Bill woke to find Rev. Eli and Little Bud, the doctor, paying their daily visits. The docter warned Bill about sitting around and not taking enough exercise. "Looks like you have given up. Every time I come, if you aren't in bed, you are sitting by one of those windows. I want you to get out some, walk around the block. Bill, exercise in moderation will help you. You don't just give up with a heart condition. You fight."

Bill smiled and promised to take a walk around the block every morning. Looking at the expression on his face as he forced a smile, one could readily see the old professor knew when he was licked.

After the doctor left, Bill and Rev. Eli, who considered Bill an authority on most subjects, discussed the race problem since one of the districts in the State had sought admission of the Negro pupils to white schools. "What do you think about it?" Rev. Eli asked.

"Rev. Eli, this is my first year out of school work and I wish to remain out, not even giving an opinion on any matters; yet, as I have always said, I feel that the Negro should first be proud of his African heritage and refuse to integrate, but build and seek for himself a place in life's rising sun. He should do this

112

by helping lessen misunderstanding and fear among all people. His work should be based on the essential worth of each individual and the power of love to overcome hatred, fear and prejudice. He should work to promote interracial and industrial understanding so that all people will have an opportunity to prepare themselves for constructive service."

Rev. Eli interrupted: "You mean then, that our people should seek industrial equalization so that they can stand alone and do so with a philosophy based on respect for the personality of each individual and a belief in the power of love rather than force to overcome evil of any knid."

"Yes, Rev. Eli. That is very necessary and especially where a situation of tension exists. We have to beware of leaders who do 'great things' for us but never really accomplish anything, and by the time they have made a name for themselves and are able to accumulate material wealth on this name, they abandon the fight and cut themselves off from the people they were pretending to help and who made it possible for them to have achieved this new-found wealth and recognition."

"Brother, I see you are thinking about some of our loud-mouthed emotional leaders whom you don't hear any more," Rev. Eli said.

"Yes, we have got to chose our leaders carefully and see that they are not just for selfish purposes. They must be cool-headed, sincere and able to view both sides of a problem without jumping to conclusions without serious thoughts and plans. Leaders who can work well with others without getting hotheaded or bigheaded. Men too big to hate but small enough to love."

After talking with Bill and discussing the problems of the community, Rev. Eli prepared to leave.

"Don't go now," Bill and Eve insisted. "Stay for supper. Bill decided he would like coming down to the dining room for a change." Eve was happy because it had been several days since Bill had come downstairs. She felt and hoped that he was feeling better. During the meal hour, Rev. Eli told some of his funny jokes and Bill laughed like his old self again.

After supper he insisted on Eve's playing some of the old songs they used to sing.

"Do you remember the night I left for the service, I sang at the party 'Old Gal, Why Don't You Answer Me?' Please play just one verse of it tonight for me. It's in the cabinet to your left marked 'Tunes to Remember'."

Eve found it and played it through, Bill humming the words.

Rev. Eli knew Bill's mind was truly on bygone days when he asked Eve to play "Let the Rest of the World Go By." He seemed to be taking the last glimpse into the past and into the early years of their happy married life. Eve wondered at Bill's seemingly new-found strength. After Rev. Eli left, they sat talking late, like two young people in love. Bill reminded her of the day he first met her, how pretty he thought she was in a little calico pinafore and a little frilled bonnet. She told Bill she thought he was the handsomest man she had ever seen and tried to impress upon him that she still thought so. This night would live in Eve's memory like one long eternity, for fate with her cruel tricks was framing up on her and soon her joy would be turned into an ocean of sorrow.

The following week they rode around the country

114

side, visiting old friends. "The South is so beautiful,"
Eve said, "this time of year. The weather crisp and
cool, the tree leaves of varied colors make the woods
a picturesque view." Friendly folks along the road-
side were picking cotton and singing. They stopped
and listened to an old lady 'way out in the field,
with her headrag on and two grandchildren picking
cotton on the same row and wearing little sacks
made from meal bags, and singing "I heard of a City
called Heaven. I started to make it my home." It was
so typical of the Old South with its happy people
who know no airs, just plain, working people who
lived and shared in that vast community. All the
workers were not Negroes. There were whites, too,
picking cotton in the same field, getting along together and sharing a common interest.

Bill and Eve would surely have to visit Uncle
Simon because he was ill. When they got there, the
old man was out in the yard feeding the chickens.
He was glad to see them.

"How is Pug?" Eve asked after they had accepted
the old man's flowery greeting.

"Oh, he fine. Why he done gone tu bring in de
cows. His snake bite bout well now. He had a terrible time. You know, my son here from Connecticut.
Cum in and see John. He tell me he git homesick
last week while listening tu du radio. Said one morning some colored fellars wid washboard, tin pans
and what not played 'Dixie.' He said he was sick in
bed and when he know anything, he had jumped
outa bed and was in der middle uf de floor dancing.
He say he know hit was time tu come home den."
The old man finished with a grin.

Bill and Eve both knew what the song meant when
they had been away from home and realized the

115

meaning of Dixie to a person reared in the friendly atmosphere of its shores.

Uncle Simon showed them his mud poultice on his lame knee caused by rheumatism and told them "dat all I eber use fur my legs and I'll be ninety next june. Kin go anywhere I wanta and cut much wood as some dese youngsters."

"Fessor, you and Miss Eve outa be glad you wusn't here last Friday when der storm cume. Why I lost my old sow and four pigs. Dey got drowned in dat ditch by der pasture. Der wind cume up too quick fur me to get dem in, but I glad hit wasn't me."

Bill and Eve assured Uncle Simon that was a splendid way to view the situation. Bill and John talked a long time about conditions in the East. John, who had been away five years, told Bill he was planning to return to live.

"Why," Bill asked, "with all that freedom you have there?"

To which John replied: "Do you actually believe that? Well, I'll tell you frankly I am only working. I am not there because I have freedom. The East is a white man's country, too, and you can believe me. You won't be there long before you know it. You don't find the kindness and friendliness there you have here in the South. Every man's for self and God for all, as my mother used to say. You have advantages here we really don't have. You get help here we can't get. You know pappy's white friends when they found out Pug was bitten by a snake came to see about him. Mr. Littleton across the road was the first to reach Pug and give first aid, and then got him to a doctor at once, which in all probability saved his life. People there don't take that kind of time with you. I know. I live there."

116

Bill thought for a while and then said: "Yes, the South is growing and with growth comes progress, and we who have watched its development have to admit the true side of the matter. The Negroes here have wonderful opportunities, and many friends who will help them develop. The Negro's job is to get to work himself and seek these opportunities, find them and make good. It's up to him to work out his own problem. He has friends here who want to see him progress and will recognize him for it. He can't sit idly by and wait for the white man to do for him the things he ought to do for himself; but working for his needs, letting his needs be known, preparing his people for the responsibility we must accept when our problems are solved. It is a task he must accomplish. It must be done, not by force, for that won't work, but through the understanding of all concerned."

"Guess we should be going," Eve said, coming into the room where Bill and John were talking while Uncle Simon listened. It was his turn now and he asked, "You gwine be to de dedecasum of dat building dey name fu you next Friday?"

"Yes, I am planning to," Bill replied, and then asked him, "are you going?"

"Man, yes! All us gwine be da. I hear dey planning a powerful big time da. Football, parade and de band gwine march and play. I wouldn't miss hit for de world. Hear lota white folks gwine be da, specially dem dat know you."

Bill didn't hear the last sentence. He was thinking and looking back forty years. Yes, Bill was viewing the progress that had been made in Warrenville. He told them that it was typical of the progressiveness of the Southland and that he could see no need of

117

any forceful move that might hinder that progress for it was surely to continue with the two races working in harmony with each other.

John spoke: "I was surprised to see this place and I have been away only five years. Never seen a place improve so quickly."

Bill responded: "Yes, whenever a people wake up to their responsibility and decide to do something about it, things get done. John, the Southern man knows what's to be done and in time he will do the needed things. Time is a healer of all ills, especially when it concerns human affairs."

"I will return soon to live and, believe me, I feel like I would have done better had I not gone. Seems like most of my friends here have their own homes and I am still paying a fortune for rent and working like H—," John volunteered.

Bill laughed and said, "I see you are a little homesick."

Bill and Eve left, saying how glad they were that they had seen John, one of their old friends. He promised to stay for the dedication the following Friday.

Bill said to Eve that night, "You know the old plantation hasn't changed much. I notice the women when we stopped by the big cotton field still suckle their babies sitting on the big sheets of cotton. Their lunch baskets reminded me of the time I was a little boy, picking cotton for Mr. Lems. Those were the best biscuits, potatoes and peas I ever ate." Bill thought, then teasingly said, "Except those you cook, honey."

Eve assured him he didn't have to apologize for, after all, his mother was a good cook.

The time passed swiftly and it was time for the

118

dedication of the new building, named in Bill's honor.

Bill was very weak and said to Little Bud and his friends, "I don't think I will be able to go. I am just tired out. That's all."

' Eve heard him and joined the group upstairs in Bill's room. "Honey, you must go. The are expecting you. I mean Warrenville is turning out in crowds just to see you, and you worked so hard to see this dream come true. It is your dream we are paying homage to. It's the dream of the fine citizens of Warrenville, both white and colored. Lets us get ready. It's almost time to begin."

Bill went downstairs to the waiting car with Eve on one side and the doctor on the other. When he entered and went on the platform, the applause was deafening as they paid homage to a grand "Old Professor."

After the program came a response from Bill, who told his audience to take advantage of every opportunity for the good of their fellowmen. "Live peaceably with all men as far as it is possible," he urged. "Don't forget the heritage of your forefathers. They knew how to pray and it wasn't old 'timey' then, neither is it now. If you haven't outgrown hate, do so. It's dangerous. Learn to love and in working with people try to see their side. Don't ask for anything. Work for it. Are you willing to pay the price for the things you want? If not, it will still remain in life's showcase. Don't fight a man about his own goods, if he doesn't want you to have them. Remember, its his and if you get if by force, there is a grave possibility you won't keep it. Get something for yourselves. Make needed sacrifices to get what you need. What you want isn't always the best thing for you."

119

The people applauded and Bill continued. "You need economic stability. Yes, good jobs, good pay, a chance to develop your people so that wherever they go or are heard of, the world over will respect the Negro race."

Uncle Simon knocked on the floor with his stick, whispered to his son John, "I tell you, 'Fessor' stepping on hit now. He ain't talking like no sick man."

He was right. Bill was his old self again when he began speaking. Eve and the doctor marvelled at his strength. They did not know that an unseen, unwanted guest sat in the principal's office waiting to see him there.

Bill was presented a gold watch by the Board of Trustees. He received it in the spirit of the same humility he had shown all through the years as principal of Warrenville school. In his acceptance remarks, he said it would serve as an inspiration and a reminder of the happy days spent there.

After the service in the auditorium, dinner was served in the cafeteria and then the afternoon program began. Eve and the doctor advised Bill to go home after dinner, but he would have none of it. This was the first football game of the season and he wanted to see it. Too, he had helped organize the band that was playing so he wanted to hear it, too.

"Little Bud," the doctor, took Bill aside to the principal's office and had him sit down while he took his pulse. It was 100 and his temperature was 96. The doctor noticed Bill was sweating. He insisted on his going home. Bill refused. He sent for Eve but she failed to impress upon him the necessity of going home and resting.

"No, I am going to see it through," he told them. When the parade began, there sat Eve and Bill

120

with the doctor in the first row of the grandstand. Bill laughed heartily as the football boys, majorettse and band came on the field. It was his life, the life of the school and the community.

The game was exciting and thrilling since Warrenville was winning. Then the band played a number to the tune of "Dixie." Bill raised his hands as if to make a gesture, but he slumped on the doctor's shoulder. They rushed him into the building and to the principal's office. There in the office he had known for years sat a visitor waiting and, as they laid him on a chair and arranged to examine him, the unseen visitor slipped him away down the valley of undisturbed peace.

The tree was cut down, but like many trees in the great forest of life, its roots of understanding, love and progressive cooperation were grounded so deeply in the Southland that no outside force can destroy their productive growth in the field of human relations.

Yes, the great people of the South will and must solve their own problems in time to the best interest of all concerned.